GEMINI

Ron Stieger

*Space
Pirate
Press*

Published by Space Pirate Press. For inquiries and other titles, please visit
www.spacepiratepress.com or www.facebook.com/SpacePiratePress.

ISBN: 978-0-9978999-2-4 (paperback)
ISBN: 978-0-9978999-3-1 (e-book)

For everyone who has ever argued about who would win

There is precious little in civilization to appeal to a yeti.

Sir Edmund Hillary

Facts: 1. Ninjas are mammals.

Robert Hamburger

Castor

Chapter 1

Sitting in the control room of his ship, on the edge of the Corsa system, Herne wondered if maybe he should have thought this through a little better. He was still groggy after emerging from his suspension pod, but he was going to have to come up with a plan soon. And he knew it had better be a good one because the pirates weren't going to be easy targets.

Back on Olympia, everyone had tried to talk him out of this. Their space fleet was limited to local defense and enforcement, so they had no interstellar invasion force that they could offer him for support. They sent messages to nearby systems, but he had no expectation of a different response from any of them. Given the impossibility of maintaining control over an interstellar colony—even Earth hadn't attempted that when the first colonizing ships set out—there would be no point in any system having a large war fleet ready to send anywhere in the galaxy. Even if such a fleet existed and was willing to be sent to defeat the pirates once and for all, coordinating the timing so it would arrive at the same time as he did would have been a major, nigh impossible, logistical challenge. For all he knew, maybe someone had arrived ten or a hundred years earlier and taken care of everything for him. He felt slightly ashamed to realize that he would be disappointed if it were the case; he wanted this revenge for himself, to know that he had personally avenged Phoenix for what had been done to her, how she had been turned into a pirate that Herne had then had to kill.

This was not what he had expected when he had been enlisted as a Pirate Hunter. He had laughed it off when his friend Magellan had asked him to take a warship from Jurassia to Olympia and fight any pirates he encountered. He had engaged Phoenix only because all other ships in the system had been disabled, and she had stolen something very important to him, the Eleusinian Totem. He had killed her as a last resort, with his own ship blown up and afraid of being killed himself on the one she had hijacked. But when he had realized that Phoenix was Magellan's own niece, captured as a child but grown up into a vicious pirate herself, he knew there was no going back to his former life. He couldn't allow the same thing to happen to anyone else, not if there was anything he could do about it.

"Castor, what do you think?" Herne asked, fidgeting in his seat, in an empty control room where he had nothing to control because the em crew was taking care of everything. In fact, he was the only human on the ship, Castor and the rest of his companions all brain emulations operating behind the scenes in the quantum computing framework of the vessel. Ems were the normal way to run a spaceship, able as they were to operate for the years needed to cover interstellar distances without the aging problems of physical bodies, and Herne wouldn't have known where to start if he had needed to take over for them.

"About?" came the response, filling the room rather than coming from any single apparent source.

"What should we do here? How do we invade Corsa, defeat all the pirates, liberate all the slaves?" That was his goal, after all, the way he intended to get his revenge.

"Survive?"

"Yes, that would be good, too."

"I'm just an engineer, you know, not a war strategist."

"Don't tell me you haven't thought about it while I've been asleep. You've had, like, five hundred, six hundred years, right?"

"That's what you would have felt," Castor answered, "if you had been awake the whole time. Subjective, at my reduced processing speed, only about eighty-three. But I had my own job to do, keeping this ship operating while you were in your suspension pod. We had a couple close calls, too, so just be glad we even got here. Besides, you'll recall, I warned you this wasn't a good idea."

Herne hadn't really expected Castor, or any of the em crew on his ship, to have any answers. But as much as he was used to working alone—leading tourists on dinosaur hunting excursions on Jurassia where he was solely responsible for all their lives, and before that, being sent on solo missions that he would rather not remember—he was finding it helpful to have someone to bounce ideas off. Too late, he wished he had tried harder to recruit at least a couple of other humans back in Olympia. As it was, it was just him and the ems, and a brain emulation running on a quantum computer and communicating through ship sensors wasn't the same as a person that he could look in the eye. But Castor had helped him out once before—though he had called himself Methuselah at the time, before his exposure to the Eleusinian Totem caused what should have been an impossible em cloning and he took the name of a famous twin—so Herne felt at least some sort of bond with him.

"Okay, let's just think this through a little," Herne continued. "We can't come in guns a-blazing. We don't have that many guns, for one thing, and this system will be swarming with pirate ships. Do you think they've noticed us yet?"

"Undoubtedly, but nobody has tried to contact us. And I don't know if it will really be swarming. There's probably not more than one or two actually in the system at a time."

"Okay, but still, we can't just attack, and when they do contact us, we'll have to have a story. One that will let us get through to the planet. Can we be smugglers?"

"That may be hard to pull off," Castor answered. "The *Umbriago* definitely looks like a warship, and someone would want a cut of whatever we're bringing, which we won't be able to offer because we're bringing nothing."

"Maybe we could tell them the truth? Maybe they'd be glad I killed Phoenix?" Herne said hopefully. "After all, she had fooled them, even if it was hundreds of years ago, and now there's less competition." He did find it strange to think about how so many lifetimes could have passed for everyone on the planet, but not for him. Luckily for him, cultural and technological change had slowed down so much once humans had started spreading across the galaxy, that a person could easily sleep a thousand years in a suspension pod and still not feel too out of place when they woke up, even if it was on a new planet.

"Maybe," Castor said, "but I wouldn't expect that much trust. And they're not going to want much to do with an em-crewed ship; you know how they feel about that. Best case, they ask you politely to leave. Worst case … not so politely."

Herne knew that "not so politely" would involve his corpse floating through space, possibly after being reduced to cosmic dust.

"So what do you suggest, then?" he asked Castor.

"You'll have to go as a diplomatic envoy from somewhere, probably Olympia would be best, just in case they've been tracking our incoming vector for a while. Make it clear you're in constant communication with that system and that if your comm link is lost there will be consequences. That should at least make them hesitate before shooting at you, and if they hesitate long enough, you have a chance. And, definitely, keep the 'Pirate Hunter' thing quiet."

"No shit. Do you think I need a false name?"

"Probably safer that way. In the time it took us to get here, your name could have bounced across this arm of the galaxy and back. I doubt any other system would have intentionally broadcast it in this direction, but pirates have a way of picking up the local gossip. I just hope they don't recognize the ship and track it back to you, but I've had my team reconfigure the transponder frequencies, just in case."

Herne turned to look at his screens. There wasn't much to see outside, just the dark of space, lots of stars. A change, then, from his visit to the Olympia system, where the Dyson sphere had blocked even that. But even within the system, Corsa was different. It lacked the big gas giants of most solar systems. They had presumably knocked each other out of orbit, tearing apart most of the small planets into mineral-rich asteroid belts. Somehow one planet had survived, and in the Goldilocks zone, no less, with liquid water and a viable atmosphere clinging to the surface and easily oxygenated once some plant life was introduced. Still, it was not a particularly appealing location, and it was far enough away from Earth and the early colonies that its first settlers were further on the "rogue and scoundrel" spectrum than most. It quickly gained a reputation as a base for interstellar pirates, and most travelers were wise enough to keep their distance. Maybe someday, several millennia in the future, civilization would advance, surround systems like this one, and shut them down, but Herne didn't want to wait that long.

"Okay," he said, breaking his reverie. "Let's go with 'Tauno Tavallinen'. They might recognize it as a fake name, but if they do—well, they're pirates, so they probably don't use their real names either. And obviously, I'm not going to give them mine, to prevent them from using me as a hostage. That should pass as an excuse. Hey, maybe I could be a Nupist missionary! Traveling from the home of the Eleusinian Totem to spread the word...."

"Do the Nupists still do missionaries?"

"I don't know; I'm sure there are some that are still wandering the galaxy."

"But why would a missionary be on a warship?" Castor asked.

"Hmm … you're right," Herne answered, slapping his forehead. "And probably best not to bring the Totem to their attention anyway, in case they associate that with Phoenix, Phoenix with me, me with pirate hunting, and that won't end well for us. We'd better stick with the diplomat story, here to offer some trade deal if they will give up their piratical ways … and with a warship, just in case they try to play mean."

"And the rest of your fleet at a distance," the em added. "Not so close to be threatening, but near enough that they could get here within these people's lifetime."

"Yeah. I'm the lucky cannon fodder. Well, hopefully that will be enough to get them to let us land. Have someone wake me if they make contact."

"Are you going back into the suspension pod?"

"No, I've had enough of that. Just a nap. Besides, it's only a few days until we get to the planet, right?"

"We've begun deceleration, so about two weeks until we get in a Corsan orbit and can arrange for our landing."

"Still, that's not enough time to be worth going into suspension. I'll just help you make sure the ship is prepped."

"There's nothing you can do to help there," interrupted Castor.

"I know, I know." Herne shook his head. "I'm still used to planning expeditions myself, being responsible for all the gear and equipment. Delegating is weird. So I'll just make sure I'm prepped myself, and figure out what I'm going to do next. But first, a nap."

Herne stood up from his chair and left the control room. The *Umbriago* was very similar to the *Pandora*, the ill-fated ship that had been his introduction to pirate hunting. Not that he had spent much time active on that ship either, from the time he left suspension before entering the Olympia system to the time it was blown to pieces by Phoenix and her accomplice, Sybil. He was sure there were plenty of subtle differences between the two that he wouldn't notice, and probably more than a few not-so-subtle ones that he had missed as well. But from the outside it had the same form, a sleek central core, primarily housing the propulsion system, and the usual gyro-stabilized ring to allow him to enjoy some semblance of standard gravity as he traveled. Castor hadn't been wrong, though; there was no doubt that it was a warship. The fusion engines had more redirection ports than a transport ship, allowing for rapid changes in direction, while additional isolation buffers allowed anyone in the ring to stay at a comfortable gee level without the ring itself breaking off and being flung into space. There were visible weapons ports in both parts of the ship, the usual array of hydrogen and neutron bomb launchers, plus beam deflectors for defense. Still not enough to battle a planet, though.

Inside was what one would expect. The control room wasn't really needed for control—the em crew could be reached from anywhere on the ship, and they didn't have or need a physical presence. If Herne had brought any humans along to help him, it would have served as a central planning area, but even on his own, he felt that was the right place for that kind of work. The exercise facilities were for keeping physically fit, the cabin was for sleeping and meditation, keeping himself mentally fit, and the control room was for work. Necessary or not, it helped him to keep his life organized, so that's how he would be living for the next two weeks, unless the pirates decided to engage him sooner. Now, as he had told Castor, with his body still adjusting to being out of suspension, it was time for a nap. So when he reached his cabin, he stretched out—at least he was able to have a long enough bed, not having to compete with crewmates for cabin space—and quickly fell into a deep sleep, filled with dreams of dinosaurs wearing eye patches and peg legs.

Chapter 2

Herne's ship hovered in orbit around the planet Corsa. Everything had gone according to plan so far. As they got closer to the planet, they had been contacted by Corsan space controllers, who laughed at the name Tauno Tavallinen but didn't seem to care that he was using an assumed name. Nobody had attacked them yet, and that was what really mattered. They even offered him a shuttle down to the surface— unlike most civilized planets, there was no space elevator here —but Herne knew he'd be better off using his own. The last thing he needed was to be alone for several hours in a space capsule with several suspicious pirates. And while the *Umbriago* could land directly if necessary, it was both more efficient to leave the big, heavy ship as far out of the gravity well as possible and much safer to give the ship and its crew a head start if escape was needed.

"Okay, Castor. Keep an eye on the ship while I'm down there."

"Of course. We've got a communication beam pointed back toward Olympia in case anyone is checking. It's spewing random bits, but the Corsans should just assume it's encrypted. Maybe they'll even set some of their mathematicians to work trying to decrypt it. That would be a fun way to waste their time."

"I'll check in at least once every … what's a day on this planet? Twenty hours?"

"Nineteen-point-three-two."

"Okay, at least once every day, whatever it is. If you don't hear from me, get your weapons team to blow up some shit and get out of here."

"I'm not just leaving you behind."

"Consider it an order from your captain, then," Herne countered. "I know you never thought of yourself as a hero; you don't need to try to be one here. If I'm in trouble, I'll figure something out."

Herne got in the shuttle without waiting for a reply. He hoped that Castor and his crew would follow that order if it came to it—he didn't want to risk their lives any more than he had to—but he expected they would probably try to do something to rescue him. Not that there was much they could do. The Corsan pirates had philosophical objections to ems, so even if Herne had brought a mobile computing platform to let them physically come down to the planet to find him, they would have been destroyed immediately. And attempting a transfer from orbit without a friendly receiver would also be essentially guaranteed death. Even without physical bodies, ems didn't like the idea of death any more than humans did, so that pretty much ruled out their joining him, even if they did come up with some kind of scheme where they could help him down there.

The world below was largely brown, with none of the lush jungles that Jurassia sported or the mixture of colors that Earth and most of the other colonized planets had, whether naturally or after centuries of climate adjustment to make them more suitable for human and other Earth-evolved life. An ocean covered part of the northern hemisphere, with a small ice cap at the pole, but well above the equator, it transitioned to land. The entire southern hemisphere was desert, and the only region showing any sign of habitability was a narrow strip from where a range of snow-capped mountains offered a source of fresh water down to the ocean where those rivers ended.

Herne had a hard time understanding why anyone would bother settling here, but he knew that for some people, any hardship was worth it if it enabled the lifestyle they wanted. In this case, the lifestyle meant pillaging and plundering passing spaceships without having to answer to any authority that frowned on that sort of thing. As his shuttle descended, Herne could make out mining operations in the foothills of those mountains and even some in the desert around them, but there was only a single real settlement in the green region, the main city which the Corsan pirates used as their base. That was where Herne navigated his shuttle toward as he finished his final orbit and brought it down on a landing strip near the ocean.

Leaving his shuttle, Herne was immediately met by three bulky men in full protective gear. He could see snipers on the rooftops surrounding the landing field, and he knew there would be others he couldn't see.

"So, 'Tauno' is it?" said the man closest to him. He was the tallest, passing even Herne, though it was hard to tell how much of that was from the boots and helmet rather than the man himself. He had a scraggly beard, a mixture of black and grey, and a few long curls of similar hue could be seen poking out the back of his helmet.

"Yes, thank you for the welcoming committee," Herne replied, raising his right hand slowly in greeting. None of the Corsans moved.

"Here to discuss a trade deal with Olympia? We have no need for trade. We take what we need. We take what we want. We'll take your ship, and you'll be lucky if we don't take your life."

"As we said, my ship is in communication with—"

"Yes, with an Olympia war fleet, conveniently out of range of our sensors and that none of our raiding ships have stumbled across. How long would a message take to get there and back?"

"Two months."

"Should we keep you in prison until they confirm your story?"

"Well, I'd prefer you didn't."

"Ha! The spy would *prefer we didn't*. What do you say, Oric?"

"I say we just shoot him here," replied the pirate on Herne's left. He was the shortest of the three but looked to be the strongest, a compact mass of muscle that would only be boosted by the exoskeleton Herne was certain was built into their armor. His eyes, barely visible behind the visor that covered the rest of his face, betrayed no hint of emotion.

"Now wait, let's not forget our manners. Ward?"

"Normally I'd agree with Oric," said the third pirate, whose face was lined with scars that showed exactly what he had needed to do to rise to his position, and what he would be willing to do to rise even higher. "But we haven't had a public execution in a while. The slaves could use a reminder, and it would be nice if we didn't have to kill off one of our good workers." Both the other pirates nodded in response.

"That's good thinking," said the center pirate, and Ward smiled at the praise. "Well, Tauno, are you a good worker? What skills do you have that we could put to use here? Digging? Building?"

"What, digging my grave or building my scaffold?"

The pirates all laughed. "See, he's funny," said the leader. "He could be a house jester. And he's a good spy, too. Any less would have pissed himself by now. Come on, Tauno, call me Solomon. I run this planet. You'll be my guest, at least until I find out why you're here to spy on us."

Herne was a little shocked to realize the pirates had been joking with him, that perhaps his life hadn't been in immediate danger, though he knew that would only continue as long as they believed he posed no threat. In any case, though he had been hoping for more independent living conditions in the city, he decided he'd better go along with the leader's proposal.

"I accept your gracious hospitality," he answered, bowing deeply while still making sure to keep his hands visible at his sides and his eyes watching forward for an attack. He knew that wouldn't do any good against the snipers, but he couldn't suppress the instinct.

Herne followed them into a hyperloop transport pod. He wasn't sure why Corsa would need a hyperloop when such a small part of the world was inhabited but not bother with a space elevator and its efficiency for moving people and things on and off the planet. Though he realized that a space elevator

would actually be a highly inefficient, and potentially dangerous, way to transfer slaves down to the planet surface, even if it
was ideal for cooperative passengers and freight. At least the
hyperloop was luxurious, even more than what he had experienced on most other planets. That was to be expected, he
thought, if it was mainly used by Solomon and the other Corsan leaders rather than for mass transit.

The hyperloop rushed them underground and brought
them back up just in front of a huge building that could only
be Solomon's palace. Herne had noticed it on his descent, the
welcoming archways contrasting with the high looming towers
that had a clear line of sight to anyone who might approach it.
Beyond the outer security wall was a large open space, a no-
man's-land forming an inner edge of the city just as the desert
gave it its outer border. He could see that wall around them
now, and the fact that he hadn't noticed passing through any
security checkpoint confirmed his hypothesis that the hyperloop was for the private transportation of Solomon and other
government leaders, probably only operating if one of them
was present.

They easily passed through the inner gate, with minimal
security required for anyone that made it this far. Closer up, he
could see it was not one simple building, but a whole complex
of corridors and interlinked structures that must have occupied
at least a square kilometer. This was not a primitive tribe led by
a brutal warlord; there was apparently a massive bureaucracy
controlling all the piracy, or, at least, the planet where all the
pirates exchanged their goods and settled when they weren't
out in space.

"I'll leave you now, Tauno," Solomon said in a vast foyer.

"Ward will escort you to your quarters. You'll be comfortable there, but you are not to try to leave."

"And when can we begin our trade negotiations?"

Solomon just laughed. "When I get confirmation that you're really here for trade negotiations, we will hear what you have to offer. Until then, my people have real work to do, and I have no one I hate enough to waste their time assigned to a trade negotiation team. Now go."

Herne followed Ward to his room. As promised, it appeared comfortable. Certainly better than the dungeon cell he might have faced if his story had been less believable. Not that Herne needed much in the way of comfort; his time hunting dinosaurs in the wilderness of Jurassia had accustomed him to scant luxuries. But he wasn't going to turn it down.

"Where should I eat?" he asked before Ward could leave.

"You have a terminal at your desk. Request what you want and it will be brought to you."

With that, Ward walked out, leaving Herne alone. He knew the room would certainly be under surveillance; every move would be watched, every sound recorded. He trusted the encryption on his personal communication link, so they shouldn't be able to decode anything Castor said back to him, but he'd have to choose his own words very carefully.

"This is Tauno. I'm here. I'm safe."

"Where are you?" came the reply directly onto his inner ear, where no external sensor would be able to pick it up, or so he hoped.

"In the palace," answered Herne. "Basically under house arrest until they are ready to begin negotiations, but at least it's a nice room."

"What do you think will happen when they find out there are no negotiations?"

"I'm sure the negotiations will go fine once they start."

"What?" Castor asked. "Oh, right. You're bugged for sure. So what's your plan?"

"I'll spend my time researching," said Herne. "Hopefully, there is some information on the terminal that will help me understand what is important to them that we could offer."

"Right…. But be careful, you don't want to arouse suspicion. Start looking up information specifically on Phoenix, and they'll wonder why. You wouldn't want them figuring out who you really are."

"Maybe knowing more local history will help."

"Okay. Keep in touch, and let me know if anything starts looking bad. Not that I can help much from orbit, but at least I can nuke them if it comes to that."

Herne laughed. "None of that, now. Remember your orders."

"Yes, captain."

Chapter 3

As polite as Solomon had been, Herne knew house arrest when he saw it. It wasn't his first time, though he hoped he wouldn't have to shoot his way out like he had on Corunda, the moment that had caused him to question his previous career choice and that eventually led him to a relatively peaceful life as a dinosaur hunt guide. That was all long before he got sucked into pirate hunting, but he hoped the experience would still serve him well here.

Trapped in his room, he spent most of his time at the terminal, searching through local historical archives, keeping his searches broad enough that he hoped nobody could tell what he was really looking for: Phoenix. There was no shortage of historical accounts of successful raids on passenger ships—no official records, of course; those wouldn't be available to him—but none that he could confidently identify as the one he was looking for.

But there were other broken stories, abounding with contradictions, just as one would expect from events that had happened a millennium or two earlier; in fact, he found it amazing that they were as coherent as they were after all that time. They included plenty of bragging and boasting from those who wanted to claim, "I knew her when...," whether taking credit for capturing her and seeing her potential or for recognizing the deceit that would come later. He recognized many of the details from the story he had heard at the Olympia quarantine—possibly from her brother, as the man had claimed to be, or he might have been just a storyteller who had heard the same tales and was passing them along with his own embellishments—in any case, they talked about finding a girl trying to hide in a closet. That alone might have been a common occurrence, or at least common enough to have been recorded more than once over the centuries. But several talked specifically about a girl who was brave and determined to be a pirate herself rather than serve as a simple slave like the rest of the captives, who was a quick learner, rapidly assimilating information and methods and able to formulate strategies that few pirates could even understand, yet they nearly always worked. That, Herne imagined, couldn't possibly be so common.

Then there were the stories about her exploits after she faked her death, left the Corsans, and set out on her own, but he found nothing that he hadn't already seen on Olympia before heading out. Fourteen information ships hijacked and held until sufficient ransom was paid in the form of Universal Bitcoin; three of those appeared to have been simultaneous, but no explanation of exactly how she had managed that. A handful of passenger vessels that surrendered at her mere name, perhaps not realizing that she had no interest in slaving or that an em—as she was pretending to be—couldn't have actually boarded and captured them, or perhaps still afraid that she would take over and disable the ship, leaving them to die in the depths of space. Herne imagined that many of her more spectacular successes had been completely anonymous, and he would never find anyone attributing them to her or even admitting that they had occurred. The Eleusinian Totem theft might have fallen in that category had Herne not shown up at the right time. He still shuddered to think what could have happened if he hadn't done so. Would it really have given her the powers she hoped for? Would the parasite have dominated her or vice versa—and which would have been worse? He was glad the galaxy would never have to learn the answers to those questions.

He didn't spend all his time doing research, though. Every day, once in the morning and once in the afternoon, Herne was fetched, usually by Ward, to meet with Solomon.

"So why are you here spying?" Solomon always opened by asking.

"I'm not spying. I'm here for trade negotiations," was Herne's automatic response. He considered trying to lighten up the conversation, imagining himself saying something like, "Just for fun," and seeing if Solomon would take it as a joke. But every time, he held himself back, not willing to risk his plan, such as it was, or his life for a moment of humor.

Solomon's questions then varied, but they were always probing, looking for any inconsistency in Herne's answers or any other clue that would give away Herne's true mission. Herne had his story well rehearsed, and he sent back recordings of his own responses to Castor at the end of the day, so he could hear them repeated back and make sure he kept his own story straight.

After several days of searching, Herne found what he

really needed to know. Yes, indeed, the story of his battle with Phoenix had reached this planet nearly five hundred years earlier. How he had been given a commission as a Pirate Hunter when he left Jurassia. How she had hijacked a ship to enter the Olympia system. How she had stolen the Eleusinian Totem. How Sybil had scrambled all the local ship navigation, leaving his as the only one able to chase her down. How he had ultimately killed her and restored the Totem to its place at the center of the Eleusinian Pilgrimage.

There was nothing about what the Totem was, though; that had been successfully suppressed. The last thing the galaxy needed was more pirates trying to take advantage of its powers, so, hopefully, they would think it was just a singular scheme by a pirate they already thought of as at least partially insane. Nothing about what happened to Sybil, either. She had escaped the *Hispaniola*, but he never found out if she had somehow made it out of the Olympia system, been captured, or ultimately died alone in her shuttle from one of the myriad ways that space can kill a person.

Most importantly for his purposes, there was no video; as he expected, the key broadcasts hadn't been sent here, so the only information in the archive was second- or third-hand reports that pirates had collected from contacts or hostages. A few pictures of Herne were there, though, and since he had aged barely a year since his victory, thanks to the suspension pod in his spaceship, he would be easily recognizable if anyone were to compare. His only hope was that it had happened so long ago that no one stuck on Corsa would remember it; after all, it was just one bit of ancient history among so many, and it didn't seem to have made its way into popular entertainments.

Their aversion to ems would be helpful to his cause; had any been around at the time the messages were received, they would likely still be running now, and there would be a chance they would recognize him, even with their human-like limitations on memory, but it was much less plausible for a human to have both seen it in the archives and remember it.

With that information, after running a few additional queries so that his last one wouldn't stand out as suspicious, Herne contacted Castor back on his ship.

"So far, so good," he said. "They don't really trust me, no surprise, but they haven't killed me either, obviously."

"And Phoenix?" Castor asked.

Herne had to remind himself that his room was almost certainly bugged, barely catching himself before he blurted out anything incriminatory. "You know, our trade statistics can be really obscure. They should be much clearer if we want to extend our trade connections here."

"You're saying the Phoenix episode is obscure enough here they won't make the connection."

"Well, you're right about that."

"What's your plan now?"

"I don't know yet. I'm still trying to understand the source of their resistance to a trade deal."

"Okay, you haven't met the local resistance yet," Castor translated.

"The warlords here have the rest of the population pretty locked down. So if I can get Solomon to agree, we'll have our deal. By the way, an execution is scheduled in five days for a young man who stumbled on the slope of the mine and kicked some rocks down on an overseer below. I guess once they decided not to execute me, they needed to find someone to fill the space."

"Looks like another slave ship is en route, scheduled to arrive in three days. That could give you an opening if everyone is busy attending to it."

"Or more information could be dangerous."

"Probably not, but you're right. You'd better be extra careful down there. Do you think they'll let you leave the palace soon?" asked Castor.

"I hope so," answered Herne. "The palace is certainly lovely, but it would be nice to explore the wonderful city here."

Just then, there was a knock on Herne's door.

"I need to go," he said to Castor, and he signed off.

His door opened—Herne knew it was always unlocked, and the knock was a courtesy that he couldn't always count on —and Ward walked in.

"Come," he said, then turned and walked back out, leaving no opportunity for question or resistance. Herne followed as he knew he was expected to.

"Still a man of few words, aren't you, Ward. Are you still disappointed I'm not the one to be executed?"

Herne was rewarded with a glance back and a menacing glare, but nothing else. He didn't push it further; he knew that as long as he was under Solomon's protection, Ward would probably not be willing to start a fight. But it would be too easy for him to find—or create—a hole in the surveillance where he could make Herne look like the instigator, and while Herne would have given himself reasonable odds in a fair fight, there was no way Ward would have allowed it to be fair. And even if Herne did come out ahead, it would likely result in his immediate ejection from the planet, not necessarily in his shuttle or with all major organs still intact.

"So you're the guest?" came a bright, cheery voice behind him.

Herne stopped and looked back. A tall, blonde woman stood there in the hall, hands on her hips. He felt Ward grab his arm to pull him along.

"Now Ward," the woman continued. "He's in no rush. Solomon can wait a minute. Hush!" she said, putting one finger up to her mouth and walking closer before Ward could object.

When she reached Herne, she held out her hand to him. "Call me Gwen." As Herne took her hand to shake it, she spun it so her hand was on top of his, let her wrist bend down, and lifted it up to Herne's mouth. Herne tilted his head in confusion; he knew a kiss was expected, but he wasn't sure why or whether it would be appropriate. He almost wished that Ward would explain what was going on, but Gwen took her hand back before he could decide what to do.

"Fine," she sniffed. "I see you don't know how to treat royalty."

She spun on her heel and marched back away from them. Ward starting tugging on his arm again, and Herne let him lead him back the way they had been going. He had read about a Gwen in his research on Solomon's family, and he tried to remember whether the pictures matched who he had just met. "Was that Solomon's sister?" he asked Ward, but he got no answer, so they continued in silence.

Ward dropped him off at Solomon's office and left with barely a nod at Solomon. It really was just an office. On his first visit, Herne had expected an elaborate palace worthy of a planetary dictator, and possibly Solomon had one of those, too, for occasions when that kind of display was necessary. But this room was simply furnished, with a large, utilitarian desk and a few chairs around it. The walls were covered with generic-looking art that could have been from any planet but was probably by some local artist that had sucked up to Solomon. A small, private terminal on the desk was overwhelmed by a large one near the doorway. All in all, it gave Herne the impression of visiting a middle manager, but he wouldn't let himself be lulled into a mistake because of that.

"So why are you here spying?" Solomon started as usual. Herne saw this conversation was not going to deviate from the script.

"I'm not spying. I'm here for trade negotiations,"

"You're good," Solomon replied. "You almost look like you mean it now. You know I monitor your archive search requests, of course."

"Of course. I might hope for better treatment as a guest, but you've made it clear you don't trust me."

"So naturally you wouldn't search for anything that might cause you trouble."

"I have no desire to cause anyone trouble here. I've just been studying the local history to better understand who I'm negotiating with. As you might imagine, the stories of most planets' interactions with Corsa are … shall we say, biased."

Solomon gave a hearty laugh. "I'm sure they are. But I wonder what you really want to be searching for but don't feel safe doing so. I mean, you searched for 'Corsan defensive weapons systems.'"

"Which the archives had surprisingly little information on. But in case you do try to harm me, I wanted the Olympian fleet to have as much of an advantage as possible when they come to avenge me."

"That's not what I think. I think you put it in there to throw me off, to distract me from what you don't want me to know you're looking for."

"I told you, I'm not here to spy."

"You'd better not be." Solomon stood up and looked down at Herne, his eyes squinting beneath his bushy eyebrows. "There is something about you, though. Something that makes me wonder why my predecessors ever agreed to receive a trade delegate in the first place."

Herne tried hard to cover his surprise. He had only thought of that cover after he had arrived in the system. How had anyone prearranged his visit, and long enough ago to have been before Solomon's time? And why had they not bothered to inform him? Luckily, he thought, great minds think alike, and he had given himself the cover story that Solomon and the other Corsans had been expecting.

When he had recovered enough to be confident he could speak without betraying his own shock, he answered, "I don't know what else I can say to convince you. But like you said, they agreed to receive me for negotiations. I know you wouldn't dishonor their commitment."

"Maybe I would, maybe I wouldn't. Maybe I'll send you back out on a thousand year loop and you can spy on my many-great grandchild instead. But for now, you can go back to your quarters."

Rattled both by the revelation that someone unknown had

set the stage for him and by his curious introduction to Gwen before the meeting, Herne walked slowly back to his room as directed. He wondered if Gwen was somehow the key, if Castor had been in communication with her before their arrival, though he couldn't explain why the em would have kept it a secret. Regardless, he was going to need to learn more about that woman before making any other plan.

Chapter 4

He didn't have a chance to do further research, though, because he returned from the interrogation to find Gwen sitting in his room.

"Hello!" she stood up and greeted him. Before he could even look around the room to see what she might have touched or found, her arms were around him. Herne wondered if he should expect a stab in the back, but it appeared to be nothing more than a friendly hug. He tentatively returned the embrace and stepped past her into the room.

He wanted to ask what she was doing here, but there were only two likely answers—spying on him or trying to seduce him—and he didn't want to hear either of them. Most likely it would be a combination of the two; Solomon certainly seemed the type to put his sister up to that, though he didn't know enough about her to know if she would agree to it. Instead, he acted as if it were no surprise at all, hoping that she would say something if it was, in fact, the third possibility, that Castor had somehow been in contact with her before.

"I'm glad you came," he said, giving a little squeeze before releasing her. "I was disappointed it took so long to finally meet you."

"So you're from Olympia?" she asked, strutting around him. "It's so rare that I get to meet such a fine specimen of off-worlder. The slaves, of course, are worthless. I wouldn't touch them even if I did think they had a chance of surviving long enough for me to get bored of them. But you...." She put a finger on his chin and tilted it up so she could look down into his eyes. "You're something different. And I'm sure I won't get bored of you." She grinned, and Herne shuddered at the implication.

"I'm not here to spy on Solomon," he said, hoping to derail the conversation from where it seemed to be heading.

"Oh, I don't care if you are or you aren't. That's his business, not mine."

Herne exhaled, not daring to relax completely, but wanting to believe that she wasn't here just to continue Solomon's questions. On the other hand, she wasn't offering to help him, which seemed to rule her out as Castor's secret contact. He stepped away from her and twirled around. Nothing looked like it had been disturbed; if it had, she had done a good enough job of it that he couldn't detect it in a quick glance. He knew he had nothing incriminating—he expected Ward or one of his cronies to periodically search the room, and he didn't want anything to be picked up by surveillance—but that didn't mean there wouldn't be something she could use to embarrass him.

"Are you supposed to be here?" he asked. He looked up and twisted his head in an exaggerated manner, as if he were scanning for hidden cameras on the ceiling. He knew they weren't there, at least not visible, but Gwen might accidentally reveal where they really were.

"I can go wherever I want, honey. Do whatever I want. Solomon and I have an … understanding." She paused as if she were waiting for Herne to ask what the understanding was, but he remained silent. "No, I won't do anything to undermine him, so leave me out of your spy games. I've got my own games in mind."

She had trapped him in the corner of the room, a quarry with no way to escape. "Can we play later?" he asked. "Right after Solomon's interrogation is not an easy time for me. Perhaps I'll see you here this evening?"

She snapped straight up, spun away from him, and strutted toward the door. "Okay," she said as she waved her hand over her shoulder. "This evening it is."

Herne waited until his door was closed and he was sure she wasn't going to change her mind and come back in. Then he contacted Castor.

"I need some advice," he started. He knew he had to be especially careful now. Anything he said about Gwen would probably get back to her, and he wanted to keep her on his side, as much as that was possible. "And you're not the best one to ask, but you're the only one I can ask."

"What is it?" Castor answered.

"Remember the thing I was searching for yesterday, about establishing *sister* cities on different planets?"

"About what? Oh, Solomon's sister, Gwen. Is she becoming a problem? Is she on to you?"

Coming on to me, thought Herne. He racked his mind, trying to think of a way to get his message through. "Never mind. Let's talk about chess. I was thinking about how powerful the queen is, especially when you're close to mate."

"Sorry, I'm not following."

Herne decided the dissembling wasn't worth it. She would just have to know he was talking about her if she wanted to. "How badly would it mess up the trade negotiations if I slept with Gwen?"

Castor waited long enough to respond that Herne thought maybe something had happened to the ship. "Um, I don't think that's a good idea. Surely, you can get access some other way."

"It's her idea, not mine."

"Well, it's been a long time since I've had to worry about that, you know."

"I know," Herne sighed. "I told you, you weren't the best one to ask. I guess I'll just have to see what happens."

"Anything new with Solomon, though?"

"No, he's still suspicious. I'll just have to be patient until he accepts that I'm no spy."

"Well, good luck. With both of them."

All Herne could do was wait. He knew there would be no useful information he could find through his terminal. On another planet, he would expect to see all kinds of theories about exactly how crazy someone in Gwen's position was, gossip and rumors that would help him know what to expect. On Corsa, though, trying to publish anything like that would lead to immediate death. He wandered around the hallways, went to the workout room to build up a sweat, took a shower, and ended up pacing around his room, still waiting.

Finally, she arrived.

"Hello, Tauno," she said, sounding very serious, almost grim. Her demeanor was completely unlike what Herne had seen earlier in the day, and Herne wasn't sure how to react to that. "Mind if I come in?"

He had a mind to say no, but he was afraid that would not turn out well for him. "Yes, please do," he said instead.

She walked past Herne sitting in the chair by his terminal and leaned against the window. "Tell me about Olympia," she said. "And anywhere else you've been."

Olympia. Herne struggled to remember anything about his short time there. "I … it wasn't much different from here."

Gwen laughed. "Really? You expect me to believe that it's as bad as this shithole planet?"

"Well, I can't really say. I've never seen outside the palace, other than from my shuttle as I was landing."

"I'll fix that for you. Believe me, though, it's crap. Now, what's Olympia really like?"

"Grand. That's the best word for it." He tried to imagine it in his head. "Looking back on it as I left the space elevator, I could think of nothing more than how much I looked forward to returning." That wasn't entirely true, but it was possible he could end up going back to Olympia and Eleusis if he was successful on Corsa.

Gwen sighed wistfully.

"The elevator itself was incredible," Herne continued, "but the whole city was like nothing I've seen anywhere else." That wasn't entirely true, either; if he went back far enough, he had been in similar cities on other planets. But compared to Jurassia, it certainly was immense, and he was pretty sure this was what Gwen wanted to hear. "I say 'the city,' but it had started out as three separate colonies. By the time I left, though, they had grown so much they nearly merged." That part he had read in the history books. "I can only imagine what it's become now."

She spun around and gave Herne a sultry look. "Take me," she said.

"What?" Herne blushed.

Gwen laughed. "Take me with you. You're not going to have any success on your mission here, whatever it actually is. Tell Solomon you're going to leave, and I'll make sure he lets you go. Just bring me along."

"Why don't you just join a pirate crew?"

"Arrr! Can you imagine?" She laughed again. "No, no captain would let me onboard. They'd be too worried about competing authority. And no crew would want to follow a captain without any experience. I'm stuck here until some tall, handsome stranger comes to rescue me." She batted her eyelashes at Herne and smiled. "When my brother kicks the bucket I might be able to run the joint, but you know that suck-up Oric isn't going to just let me have it."

"You want me to go home as a failure?"

"Come on, it's not like anybody will actually remember you. 'Random person returns from Corsa alive' would actually be fairly newsworthy on its own. Or are you talking about your so-called 'war fleet' that's waiting just beyond our view? We can wipe them out, if you don't want them embarrassing you. They're not really there, though, are they?"

Herne tried to keep his face as steady as possible, so as not to betray himself. "I have to see the town here first. If I'm just going to leave, I at least want to be able to say I visited more than the inside of this palace, as splendid as it is."

"I can make that happen," Gwen said, jumping away from

the window and onto Herne's lap, causing him to jerk back in surprise. "Just think of all the fun we'll have on a spaceship together." She leaped up just as quickly and walked out without another word, leaving Herne completely befuddled but hopeful that she would come through on her promise to get him more freedom.

Chapter 5

After the next day's visit with Solomon, Herne was allowed to leave the palace compound and walk through the streets of the city. He didn't see Gwen that day, but he assumed that she was behind his new privileges, and he wondered what price he would have to pay for it. He planned to leave as early as he could, so that he could be alone on his first exploration and avoid any difficulties if she were to insist on accompanying him.

He enjoyed the pre-dawn light and the quiet, which he could never experience in the palace, with security always bustling around. The town was filled with small shops—all closed at this hour—which Herne looked forward to visiting later in the day, or in future days, assuming he continued to have the freedom to explore. He would come back with Gwen as a guide to explain the local arcana that he wouldn't notice or understand himself, but he wanted his first experience to be independent.

The architecture was … unique, was the best way he could think of to describe it. It looked like many of the buildings were actually made of wood, which would be unusual on any planet but even more so on one like this where trees were sure to be a rare commodity. He knew it wasn't real wood, of course, though perhaps the rarity was what had inspired the look when the architects designed the structures. There were odd curves in many of the roofs, evoking thoughts of seagoing vessels swaying in the high winds which often blew down from the mountains, stirring up swirls of dust in the streets. The iron railings on the balconies at least made sense given the local materials, though he rarely saw anyone actually using those balconies.

As he walked and looked around, he thought about what his next steps could be here to destroy the pirate leadership. He knew he couldn't expect an obvious opportunity to pop up, but he was keeping his eyes open for any lead that he may be able to follow up on later, a hint of a subversive group meeting in the town or a nascent coup being plotted within the palace. His mind was deep into these thoughts when a bag came down over his head, and as he tried to spin around, his arm was grabbed and pinned behind his back.

"My name is Tauno Tavallinen! I'm here on a diplomatic mission!" he tried to yell, but the bag muffled his voice. Herne didn't know whether his attackers were sent by Solomon—maybe he wasn't being trusted after all—or if they were mere street thugs. "I'm under the protection of Lord Solomon!" That wouldn't help him if Solomon had sent them, of course, but it was the only chance he had. Still, he got no response other than finding himself driven off the street and into the nearest building. Herne was by no means a small man, and he hadn't lost any of the strength that had made him an excellent dinosaur hunter on Jurassia, but he was no match for the nameless, invisible person behind him.

Inside, he heard the door slam; his arm was released, and he was shoved into what he presumed was the middle of the room. He quickly ripped the hood off his head and turned around, but the room was pitch black and he could still see nothing.

"Who are you? Where am I? What do you want with me?" He fired out questions in all directions, but no response came.

He braced himself for a new attack, not knowing where it would come from but expecting it any second. He quieted his breathing, listening carefully to get as much warning as possible, but he couldn't hear a sound.

Finally, a whisper came from across the room: "Herne Sutherland."

He whirled around, hoping the darkness would hide the shocked look that he couldn't keep off his face after hearing his real name here. Now he knew he was in real trouble, his cover broken. He wondered if it was worth trying to communicate with Castor, but he didn't want to give away anything yet, not knowing exactly how much they knew. And there must be a lot they didn't know, or they would have simply killed him already. Besides, if his captors were careful, they surely would have made certain this safe house was electromagnetically shielded, preventing him from reaching any external assistance. He knew an answer was expected, though, and he decided silence was the best response; if they weren't going to answer his questions, he didn't need to offer anything back.

"Herne Sutherland," the voice came again, somewhat louder this time. "We know who you are. Speak."

"If you think you know who I am, I should know the same of you. I say nothing else until I know who I'm speaking to."

"Call me Rila."

"Okay, Rila." Herne turned slightly, hoping he could at least identify which direction the voice was coming from. "My name is Tauno Tavallinen. I don't know who this Herne Sutherland is or why you think I'm him. What does Solomon want with me?"

"Herne Sutherland." The voice seemed to be coming from all over the room, every word apparently from a different direction. "What is your relationship to Solomon?"

"I am under his protection. I am on a trade mission from Olympia. If you want to know more, ask him yourself."

"Herne Sutherland. We know what you did in Olympia." Now the voice was louder and seemed to be coming from all directions at once. *We*, it said; of course it wasn't a single person.

"Who else is here, Rila? Why don't you just tell me what you want?"

"What is your relationship to Solomon? Did he send you to kill Phoenix?"

Herne's mouth gaped open. This was not the question he was expecting, and it wouldn't be a question any of Solomon's men would have asked.

"You think you know who I am. Let me see you! Tell me what you want."

The lights flashed on brightly for a moment, forcing Herne to close his eyes before he could get a good look at anything. By the time he opened them, it was completely dark again. Had he seen a person in front of him? He reached out and took three steps forward, then heard a voice scream immediately behind him.

"Tell us your relationship to Solomon!"

Herne ducked down, spun around and lunged, but hit only empty air. He heard a crack as something very solid hit the back of his head, and he fell to the ground and passed out.

* * *

When Herne woke back up, he found a bottle of some liquid in his hand. His mouth was parched—how long had he been out, he wondered—so he opened the bottle, smelled it carefully, and, hoping it was just water, took a sip. He wasn't afraid of poison; there would have been easier ways to kill him while he had been unconscious. Or before that, he realized, given how poorly he had put up a fight. But it could be laced with any kind of chemicals that could put him into a more pliant mental state. On the other hand, they could just as easily have injected him with those drugs while he was out, and he needed to drink something.

As if the action of drinking had triggered a motion sensor, he heard the quiet voice again: "Herne Sutherland."

Herne sighed. "Yes, fine. Call me Herne Sutherland."

"What is your relationship to Solomon?"

"I have no relationship with him. He met me when I landed two weeks ago and has kept me under house arrest since, assuming I am a spy."

"Did he send you to kill Phoenix?" The voice remained quiet; apparently, as long as he was answering, Rila felt no need to raise their voice. The sound echoed in his ears in such a way that he wasn't sure if it was an intentional effect or merely a result of his concussion.

"I told you! I just met him! He couldn't have sent anyone

to kill Phoenix anyway." Herne tried to stay on safe ground here, only giving away information that they should know already. "That was … I don't know how many hundreds of years ago. At most, it would have been his predecessor, some-one far back in the dynasty. I don't even know who that would have been."

Herne could feel the silence return and waited to hear how they would react to this. After a long stretch, the voice came back.

"Herne Sutherland. Pirate hunter. You have one chance to answer this truthfully: why are you here?"

Herne paused, considered all the answers he could possibly give. They clearly weren't going to believe he was here on a trade mission, so he settled on the simplest truth he had: "Revenge."

"Revenge on whom?"

"Revenge on the pirates who kidnapped a little girl." Herne gained strength as he said this, reminding himself of his mission. "Who forced her into a life of piracy. Who led her to die at my hands."

The lights started to come on, this time gradually enough that his eyes could adjust. Five people moved toward him slowly from the edge of the room, which was otherwise empty. All five were dressed in black bodysuits, faces covered and barely distinguishable from one another.

"Good answer, though I hope you understand why we had to be sure of your intentions, Herne Sutherland. You may con-tinue to call me Rila." Herne turned to face the speaker, clearly female in the tight clothing, though the voice remained gender-less. "My colleagues here you may also call Rila, or not, as you choose." The others all bowed as one. "Nobody else will know us by that name, so if we hear it, we will know you have betrayed us. You do not know us. Not personally, not our organization. Few who do live, and if you speak of us, you certainly will not. But we can help you achieve your goal. If you help us."

"What is your 'organization?'" Herne asked, happy to finally have a chance to ask a question of his own.

"We will not tell you that. We will tell you our mission: political revolution here on Corsa. We can also tell you that Solomon's ancestors have been leading this planet and supporting its pirates since long before the time of Phoenix's capture, back all the way to shortly after the first settlers here, when his clan emerged as the victor in a vicious battle between warlords. Probably even more interesting to you, his right-hand man, Oric, is the son of the pirate captain that led the raid on Phoenix's ship."

"Son? Not many generations?"

"No," Rila answered. "Captain Arjis led some of the furthest reaching space missions, and he retired here only forty years ago. He promptly chose a slave girl as his wife and impregnated her, as he did every time he returned to Corsa. The poor girl was executed as soon as she gave birth, and the child was raised by another slave, this one executed at Oric's own hand once he came of age."

"And does Arjis still live?"

"Yes. He lives in the palace complex in the same wing as your quarters, one floor above you. He is old and weak now, but still respected for his past exploits."

"Great!" Adrenaline was pumping through Herne's body

now, and he was ready to leap up, the shock of the earlier attack completely forgotten now. "Tell me what he looks like, so I can kill him."

"No. Not so simple. You can have your revenge after you help us."

"And how do I do that?" The room was no longer looking so nondescript to him. Though still empty of furnishings and dimly lit, he was able to notice some of the details of the architecture. The rigid lines dividing all the walls into rectangles, not a single arch to be seen. The smoothness of the dustless floor. The sliding panels that led to other rooms, meaning perhaps this was a normal home, not simply a convenient empty warehouse.

"You live in the palace complex," Rila brought his attention back to her proposal. "We need you to infiltrate their core security systems. It's not enough to kill one man, not even Solomon. Or one woman either, because his sister Gwen has as much power as he does. We are here to destroy the entire Corsan leadership and free the slaves."

Herne again had to hide his shock; what exactly did Rila mean by Gwen having as much power as Solomon? She had always talked about having nothing to do with politics, but maybe she had been trying to manipulate him. But if Rila didn't know about his relationship with Gwen, that meant her information wasn't perfect, and he wasn't going to change that. "And you are going to do that with five people? Okay, six, if you count me?"

"Our organization has done more with less. We know what we're doing. But we need someone on the inside, to help us get started."

"Sure, whatever," Herne sighed. "I guess I don't have much choice. Tell me what you need me to do."

"In the subbasement, you'll find the security control room. Here's a safedisk with the building layout, including camera monitor locations and internal passcodes." Herne took the disk from her hand and pocketed it. "You will need to memorize it, and if you get caught with it, it will mean certain death for you. In four days there will be an execution." Herne nodded; he knew about that already. "One hour before it is scheduled, get to that room and disable the external security. We will do the rest."

"How do I get into the security room without getting caught?"

"That's for you to figure out. If you succeed, we implement our plan. We will save Captain Arjis for you if you like. If you fail, we wait for the next opportunity. It will not include you."

Herne caught the threat in her voice. It wasn't only Solomon who would be planning to kill him if he failed. He glanced around and knew that the others were all looking at him with the same threat in mind, even if he couldn't see it behind their masks. "Nice. Don't worry about Arjis. If you accomplish your goal and there is no more piracy out of Corsa, that will be enough revenge for me."

"Good. Now, do you have a local credit card?"

"Of course," Herne answered. As Solomon's guest in the palace, he hadn't had to pay for anything, but he had been prepared when he shuttled down from the *Umbriago*.

"How much is on it?"

Herne thought for a moment to remember what he had

arranged. "About ten thousand UBC. I can download more from my ship if I need to."

"Give it to us," Rila said, holding out a hand

"What? Why? Do you really need the money?" Despite his confusion, he removed the card from his pocket and handed it over to Rila.

"We can't just let you walk out of here. If you had been more cooperative early, maybe, but now it's been too long. There will be too many questions asked. You were robbed by local thugs—there are plenty here, trying to prove themselves strong or violent enough to earn a place on a pirate ship crew, so it's believable. They took your credit card, beat you up, and left you lying in the street."

Herne hesitated a second before the meaning sunk in. "What? You mean…?"

But he didn't have a chance to finish his question before one of the others, who had crept up silently behind him, knocked him on the head again, causing him to black out before he even hit the floor.

Chapter 6

After Herne's supposed mugging, Solomon had confined him to the palace again, for his own safety, of course. Unfortunately for Herne, that meant he still hadn't had the opportunity to fully explore the town as he had hoped to. At least having been beaten up so badly by what he said were mere street crooks made him look less like a master spy and seemed to reduce Solomon's suspicions. Gwen, on the other hand, became more attentive than ever.

"I'm so sorry I let you go!" she had wailed when he first returned. Herne had tried to comfort her, reminding her that he had practically begged her to get him out of the palace. She wrapped her arms around him, and he didn't know whether the embrace was that of a lover or a miser jealously guarding her possessions. Or, remembering what Rila had said about her, was it the grasp of a chessmaster, holding onto the piece she was going to move next, perhaps to sacrifice. Whatever the reason, she rarely gave him a moment alone, even taking over for Ward in escorting him to Solomon. He feared to fall asleep in his own room with her there, lest a secret slip out, but four days of making sure she didn't get bored left him little time for sleep anyway.

Since there was no way he could safely analyze the palace layout himself, he uploaded the contents of the safedisk to his ship. There, Castor and any ems in the crew that were good at this kind of thing could figure out the best way to get the security systems disabled as he had promised Rila he would. They could also take advantage of the ship's regular computing facilities, while Herne couldn't very well run anything related to this on the terminal in his own room. He knew he wouldn't be able to discuss it in detail over his communicator, either, so he had to trust his crew to envision a viable plan for him to implement. They came through the morning of the execution, with a strategy so straightforward that it seemed too easy.

The internal security cameras were the easiest part, as he didn't even have to evade most of them. He was free to walk around the upper levels, so any guards monitoring them would be used to seeing him and know he wasn't a risk. Plus, he had become a regular in the workout facility, and that was one of the few places he could be away from Gwen. He had already been varying which stairwell he used to return to his own room, which gave him flexibility for starting out. Those stairs also continued down to the subbasement, with one of them opening right next to the security control room, and he knew there were no cameras watching the stairs themselves, only the doors leading to them. Entering the stairwell would be no problem; he would just appear to be going down one level to his room. He would be quicker than usual descending the stairs, in case a careful watcher noticed that he didn't emerge where he was expected, and then he would stumble out at the subbasement level as if disoriented.

If he was lucky, a single guard would come out of the control room, assuming he was ill and needed assistance. With a spasm, he would throw something—he hadn't yet decided what exactly—apparently at random but in fact carefully aimed to disable the camera that would be watching him. He would then need to overpower the guard, unlikely to be too challenging given the element of surprise on his side, and enter the control room itself. He didn't know how many security personnel would be in there—the shift information he had was only partial—but he hoped it would be light, with the need for extra security presence around the execution site leaving only a minimal force within the palace. If that was the case, he might be able to make his move and get back out without being noticed as anything more than a sick man posing no threat to anyone. In the worst case, all he needed was a moment if he timed it right; as long as Rila and company came as promised, they would be his backup plan if he wasn't able to get out on his own.

Two hours before the execution—one hour before he had promised Rila the security systems would be disabled and thirty minutes after Gwen had given up trying to convince him to attend with her—Herne headed up to the workout room for the first step of the plan. This was actually what he liked best about it; the adrenaline from the exercise would heighten his senses and speed his reactions. The room was empty as he had hoped, with everyone from the palace attending the execution, leaving him free to run through the rest of the plan in his head without distraction. Fifteen minutes before he needed to leave, however, an old man walked in.

"You're Tauno, right?" the man asked.

"Yes," Herne huffed, speeding up the treadmill in the hope

that he wouldn't be drawn into a conversation that he didn't have time for.

"Call me Arjis," the man continued.

Herne had to struggle to prevent his shock from showing on his face. "Why aren't you at the execution?" he asked.

"I've seen enough. Killed enough myself. They never had to execute mine, you know. I could tell whether they'd be trouble, and I got rid of those ones right away. There's no pride anymore; they just bring them all here and make them someone else's problem. Nobody even cares if I show up now. But you're a foreigner, and I know you've been studying our history. If you really want to learn what's important to us, you should go. I'll even take you."

"No. I'd really rather not." Herne was counting on the heavy breathing and elevated heart rate from his running to mask anything that in other circumstances might have betrayed his stress level.

"Actually, I insist," Arjis said firmly.

Herne looked at the clock. He still had twelve minutes before he was supposed to head to the security room. Arjis was acting as if he suspected something, though Herne couldn't imagine how this man he had never met could have learned something that Solomon and Gwen hadn't. He couldn't take the risk of Arjis following him downstairs, though.

"Give me time to wash up. Meet me at my room in fifteen minutes, and we can go together."

"Five minutes," Arjis countered. "I'm an old man. I don't move too fast, so I need all the time I can get to reach the killing ground."

Herne didn't have much choice now; he'd have to do it

early and hope that all the security gates stayed open long enough for Rila to take advantage of it. He had no way to notify them he'd be moving early, and he didn't know how they could tell whether he had been successful, so there was a risk they would miss the moment, but there was nothing he could do about that now.

"Fine," Herne said, and he jumped off the treadmill and ran for the stairwell. He was glad he had already picked up a dumbbell and hidden it under his towel before Arjis had arrived.

He rushed down the stairs as fast as he could, dropping the towel along the way. As he reached the subbasement level, he thought he heard an upper door opening. Had Arjis followed him to the stairs rather than taking the lifts and meeting him as planned? He didn't have time to worry about that now; he just had to proceed with the plan. Doing his best to fake a seizure, he fell against the door handle and pushed it open, collapsing in the hallway.

Sure enough, one guard exited the security room to check on him, but before Herne could make his move, there was Arjis at the bottom of the stairs himself. Maybe he was not as much of a slow, old man as he pretended.

"What is this? Careful," Arjis said to the guard, "that man was fine less than a minute ago. This seems like a trap. Call for backup and don't take your eyes off him."

Herne knew there was no way he could keep up this charade under close inspection. His whole plan had relied on superficial appearances and fast decision making. He thought about attacking Arjis with the dumbbell, but he knew that would make his situation worse. As the guard backed away, leaving him lying on the floor propping the door open, Arjis turned to Herne.

"So, Solomon was right at first! You are a spy! What should I do with you now? Crush your skull under my heel? I'm still strong enough, you know. Or have the guard shoot you straight out? No, both of those would be far too private, and Gwen will want to hear exactly how you betrayed her. She should have known better. I warned her, she just laughed and told me to stop begging. As if I needed to beg for her. A pity we already have an execution scheduled today, and we like to spread those out, keep them fresh in everyone's mind. It will be up to Solomon, though."

Several more guards came out from the security room then. Two of them kept their distance, with guns drawn and pointed directly at Herne, while another joined the original guard and forced Herne to stand up, shackled his wrists and ankles together, and marched him down the hall, through the security control room, and into a tiny cell. Through all of this, Arjis's glare was focused directly on Herne's face, and his taunts echoed through the hallway until the heavy door closed and separated Arjis from the target of his scorn.

"This is all a misunderstanding!" Herne tried to explain to his captors. "I am a guest of Solomon's! I don't know what that man was talking about, calling me a spy. I just met him a few minutes ago," he continued, but the guards paid him no attention.

After several minutes, Herne accepted the fact that his pleas would be ignored, and he would have no one willing to listen to any explanation until Solomon or Gwen returned from the execution. He tried to sit down, but the cell was far too narrow; the best he could manage was leaning against the wall with his feet propped against the bars, and that was even more uncomfortable than standing. He had to keep his hands off the bars, though, lest he cut himself on the rust; this cell clearly didn't see much use, and no one cared much about maintaining it. He figured few people that might qualify for imprisonment here avoided being shot directly; probably his status as Solomon's guest was the only reason he was still alive to stand in this dark, decaying corner of the security room. He tried to find some angle to see the control board—thinking that if he did survive the day, at least some good might come out of his capture—but the cell was around a corner and didn't give him room to move his head far enough to see anything useful beyond it.

Time passed. Herne grew thirsty, as he always was after a hard workout, but his requests for water were ignored just as his earlier protestations had been. His skin felt clammy from the sweat, and the salt was beginning to sting his eyes, but he didn't even bother complaining about that. At least if he was getting dehydrated, he wouldn't have to piss himself, or so he hoped, with no idea how long he'd be forced to stand there. He didn't even have a good sense of how quickly time was passing; he had tried counting his breaths and heartbeats once he gave up on getting anyone to answer him, but he lost track after only a few minutes, and of course they had confiscated his watch before leaving him here, not taking a chance that he might use it to communicate with anyone on the outside.

Finally, as he was just about to let his head rest on a hopefully not too rusty section of metal and possibly fall asleep, he heard the door to the security room open. The guards all jumped out of their seats, but the footsteps continued past them and around the corner until he could see Solomon on the other side of the bars from him.

"So, why are you here spying?" Solomon asked, with an intensity that Herne hadn't heard since his first day here. Over time, Solomon's opening question had turned into a kind of running joke, one he never expected an answer to but still felt necessary to ask, but not anymore.

"I'm not spying. I'm—" Herne tried to answer, but an electric shock went through the bars he was holding. Once it had stopped and he could relax his muscles, he quickly felt for the rusty spots, hoping for enough insulation to justify the cuts they might cause on his palms.

"Usually I'm in a good mood after an execution, but today they came and told me they had caught you skulking down here. So I only have one question to ask today, and I will keep asking until I hear an answer I like. Why are you here spying?"

"I'm not—" The current came again, and the rust didn't seem to make much of a difference. "Wait," Herne continued when he could. "Let me finish."

"Why are you here spying?"

"I'll answer. Really, I'm not here spying. But—"

"But what?" Solomon yelled. "And you better not be about to mention trade negotiations, or I'll leave the bars charged all night and find you barbecued by morning."

"Not spying. Revenge." Herne hoped the truth would work as well here as it had with Rila, and that he wouldn't have to share the whole truth.

"Now that's interesting." Solomon came closer and stared right into Herne's eyes. "Who are you seeking revenge on?"

"Not you."

"Good answer."

"Arjis. He captured her. Long ago."

"Arjis, yes, he's the one that caught you out today. Seems like you have another reason to hate him now. But who is this he captured that you're so eager to avenge?"

"Phoenix," said Herne.

"Phoenix? I don't recognize that name."

"She became an em."

"Oh, I think I've heard that story." Solomon turned and spat. "Nasty ems. I don't see how any planet can call themselves civilized when they give up the responsibilities of humans to those ... things. So she made herself a sub-human before she died, I can see why you'd be upset about that, and you blame Arjis for taking her away and leading her to that. What was she ... your wife? Daughter? Lover? Sister? All of the above?" Solomon sneered.

Herne knew that Solomon only had half of Phoenix's story, but he was in no hurry to fill in the gaps or reveal his own role in it. "Niece of a friend."

"Wow. Pretty distant relationship for you to go through all this trouble."

Now, Herne thought, was the time to bring his cover back. He hoped he had shared enough of the truth that Solomon would buy it. "No trouble. I am a trade negotiator. Convinced Olympia to try you. Got myself assigned. Thought I could make deal, kill Arjis, be gone. Or even if no deal, still kill Arjis."

"You couldn't though, could you? You couldn't even go one day in the city without getting robbed, so I don't know how you thought you could manage killing an experienced captain like Arjis. But I do appreciate your honesty, even if it comes so late. So I won't have you killed right away. You'll march off to the mines while I send a message to your Olympian fleet giving them my ransom demands. And if that fleet doesn't exist or doesn't respond, then I'll march you right back here, and you'll get to be the next execution."

With that, Solomon turned and walked away, leaving Herne to ponder what a lifetime of slavery would feel like, along with how short that lifetime would actually be for him.

He didn't have long to himself until he heard someone else barge into the security room.

"Let me at him!" he heard Gwen's voice shouting.

"What were you thinking?" She looked like she wanted to reach through the bars and strangle Herne herself, but she pulled her arms back to herself at the last second. "Arjis was right about you. I thought he was just jealous because I had gotten bored with him. He thinks he can have anyone he wants just because he's an old pirate captain. The fact that you were a newcomer, the kind of person he would normally have captured or killed, made it worse for him, I think. But he was right! You came just to use me! Why? Who told you to do this?"

Herne wanted to remind her that she was the one that seduced him, but he didn't think that would help his cause at the moment. Instead, he took a step back from the bars, worried about how much of a shock Gwen might try to apply.

"Not even an answer!" she continued her rant. "No explanation, no apology! I could kill you, you know. Not just have you killed—I'd do it myself. Come back when you're asleep and slice a knife through your neck, just enough to wake you and let you bleed out. No one here would dare help you. But the mines are better for you. I visit them all to supervise the torture sometimes. You'll wish I had done it here."

She turned and stomped away silently. Herne thought he heard a sniff and maybe a sob as she left, but he knew that could have been as much for show in front of the guards as real emotion.

Chapter 7

Shortly after Gwen left, Herne was removed from the tiny holding cell. He was savvy enough to not expect an improvement in his situation, so he wasn't disappointed when he found himself taken directly to a larger, more crowded version of the same, with a hundred or so prisoners and slaves to keep him company. The guards told him nothing, not how long he would be staying there, where he would be going next, or what any of the others were there for.

None of his companions were talking either. He had room to sit on the floor, but not enough to stretch out and lie down, and he wasn't one of the lucky few that had secured a spot by a wall. Instead, he sat back to back with a woman who could balance his weight, but even so, his ability to sleep under nearly any conditions was going to be tested to its limits. Between the wailing of many of the other captives, the stench from so many people packed so closely together, and the fear of what would happen to him when Solomon realized there was no Olympic fleet, he would be lucky for even a few minutes of actual sleep. He hoped that Castor would do the sensible thing and clear out while he could, but he had no way of knowing what was happening up on the ship. And he had no hope that Rila and her organization would do anything to save him; he had failed, and they would just wait patiently for their next opportunity, whether it would take years, decades, or even centuries to come.

When morning came—or, rather, when the guards came, for Herne had no idea when the morning had actually begun —he was still awake, and still alive, which was more than he could say for three of his unfortunate companions. He didn't know who they were; no one in the cell had shown any interest in their neighbors beyond staking out their own space, and Herne knew better than to be the only one asking questions.

"Everyone out!" The guards opened the gates, and Herne watched as some of the prisoners, including his erstwhile pillow and everyone near the corpses, hurried for the exit. Others hung back, wary of what worse tortures might await them once they departed. There was a cacophony of shouting from the early goers—elbows were thrown along with more than a few punches—but that didn't last long. One of the instigators was pulled aside by the guards, pummeled until he collapsed to the ground, and then shot in the head; that was all it took for the chaos of the crowd to subside.

Herne himself proceeded cautiously but stoically once the initial rush was over, with a feeling of relief once he was out and had space to move around a bit. Another prisoner pushed her way past him, trying to make a run for it. Herne never knew if she thought she could actually make it or was simply hoping for a quick death; either way, that was what she got, as three guards simultaneously shot her down. Gradually, more of the prisoners exited and were shackled together by the guards, until only a few remained. Two of the guards entered the cell at that point, yanking out the laggards one by one and shooting the dead ones, just to be sure.

"Follow us," cried one of the guards when the prisoners were all locked together. "And not a word out of any of you."

The halls they were led through were otherwise empty, a direct path from the prison to the courtyard of the palace complex that nobody would want to find themselves accidentally in the middle of, lest they get mixed up with the prisoners. He had thought the hallways on the upper floors had been severely undecorated for a palace, but this area was bare concrete all around. Herne counted three sets of heavy security doors they passed through as the corridor sloped upward from the underground cell to the exit. When they emerged in the growing daylight, he saw again the snipers stationed on the outer wall. This time, unlike during his arrival, many of them were aiming down at him and his companions rather than watching for intruders from outside. Herne worried that the slightest thing —a prisoner tripping on loose gravel, a stray reflection mistaken for a weapon flash, a single word of frustration and fatigue—could lead to an unintended slaughter. He prayed that none of the other prisoners would be so foolish as to do anything but follow passively where they were led.

There was no chance of using the hyperloop, of course, but at least they made it through the courtyard without incident. After they passed through the outer gate, they were marched through the town, down the same streets that Herne had seen so briefly before. Now those streets were lined with hecklers throwing insults—and occasionally rocks—at the row of prisoners. Herne tried to keep an eye open for Rila or any of her comrades. He didn't expect to see them, let alone have them launch a rescue, but he wanted them to at least know what had happened to him, that he had done his best and not betrayed them, even though doing so might have saved him from this fate.

"Where are you taking us?" a man not far behind Herne finally had the courage to ask. The question immediately earned him a whip across his shoulders, but he was also rewarded with an answer from a guard walking by Herne's side: "The Mavros mine on the other side of the mountains."

That answer was meaningless to Herne, but he could tell from the reaction of the others near him—the gasps, the shudders, the silence that was somehow even deeper than it had been before—that the locals knew what it meant. He had seen the mountains on his way down, of course, and he guessed from the direction they were marching that they weren't going to be taking an easy path along the beach and around the range. No, a mountain pass was going to be in his future, and if his estimate of the distance was anywhere close, it would be five days before they got there on foot.

No one else was interested in asking questions after that, or at least no one that Herne could hear over the jeers of the crowds. The sun rose higher, occasionally a prisoner stumbled and was shoved roughly back into line by the nearest guard. Herne tried to keep his eyes straight ahead and his pace consistent; all he knew was that this was not the street he had been on when Rila had attacked him. Eventually, the crowds thinned out, and the city ended abruptly, leaving them on an isolated road wending its way into the foothills. Somehow all the prisoners had managed to stay together without anyone starting a riot or being shot for not being able to keep up.

Several kilometers beyond the edge of the town, they came to an array of trucks. They were big, steel gray, six-wheeled beasts that looked like they could drive over a steep mountain pass as easily as a speed bump on a road. Herne heard the sighs of relief and the prayers of gratitude to various deities from the prisoners around him, but he knew better than to be too grateful. He imagined they had been marched through town to provide a spectacle, or to serve as a warning to others. But if they were being given a ride now, it was only to leave them fit for brutal labor when they reached Mavros.

"All right!" yelled one of the lead guards into an amplified bullhorn. From what Herne could tell, under the protective armor and cold weather gear, he was a short, muscular man not unlike how Oric had appeared when Herne first landed. The hint of a mustache seemed visible on his dark-skinned face, though Herne couldn't be sure it wasn't just an odd shadow from the guard's visor. "In the trucks, you'll each find your ration for the day. That's all you get until we reach the camp. If you haven't eaten by then, tough shit. If you need to piss, do it now before you get in the truck."

Herne followed his chain into the second truck, crammed in with nineteen other prisoners—all still shackled together—and three guards. He picked up what they had referred to as a ration, a textureless, pre-fab brick of what was presumably protein and fiber; it was common fare, and Herne didn't particularly mind them, though he wouldn't say he exactly enjoyed them. He found his left arm pulled away from him as the man next to him raised his own hand to his mouth, tugging on the chain between them. Herne realized he would have to do the same, mumbled an apology to the woman on his right, and took a bite. It tasted like wax—they hadn't bothered adding any of the usual flavorings to prisoner rations—but it was still food.

Once the truck was underway, Herne took a moment to look at his traveling companions. Eleven men and eight women, a wide range of ages. In fact, as he looked closer, he realized one of the men was merely a boy, certainly no older than fourteen. He searched for hints about why they were all here. Murder? Petty theft? Conspiracy? Innocent, political opponents? Or merely slaves captured from a hijacked vessel and dumped with the local prisoners? It could have been anything; no one's face betrayed the reasons, and nobody, least of all Herne, was about to start asking.

One of the guards in the back of the truck with him—a mean looking woman with clipped hair, a stubby nose, and an odd dent in one ear, Herne could see now that she had taken her helmet off in the truck—brought out a pipe, an old-fashioned one with real tobacco. She lit it and leaned back, relaxing against the back door. The nearest prisoners started to choke on the smoke—not used to it, Herne could tell, since even here on Corsa, most people that needed a stimulant fix went straight for dermal injections—but the guard paid no attention.

"Hey! Easy on that!" called the guard in the front. He was an older man, with a tired look on his face that made it seem like he was just here to do his job, not out of a love of violence and power like some of the younger ones. Herne wondered how long it had taken him to lose that, or if he had been the rare exception even in his younger days. "We're stuck in here for eleven hours. Don't be making it worse for us!"

Eleven hours, Herne thought. That was a lot longer than he had anticipated, and it was clear why the trucks had been necessary; there was no way they could have walked the whole distance. It would have been a death march for sure, with no one left to work the mine.

"I just need one to get me started," replied the smoking guard.

"Whatever, Zara," the front guard mumbled. "Jarel won't approve."

"Jarel's not going to know shit! You know you should have retired long ago, and if you cause any trouble, I'll get Jarel to leave you at Mavros. Maybe even throw you off the edge myself."

The other guard had no response to that, but everyone seemed on edge for a while, waiting to see if the argument would flare up again. He closed his eyes, though, apparently not wishing to start a fight. When the tension had dissipated, the woman to Herne's right whispered to him, "My name's Lei-tan."

"Tauno," Herne replied under his breath, after waiting to see how the guards would react to Lei-Tan's speaking. Apparently, they were okay with it, more relaxed now that they were away from the city and didn't have to worry about appearances, or maybe just from the nicotine in the air. He still wasn't about to start using his real name under these circumstances, though. He glanced over to get a better look at his new conversation partner; she was very short and thin, especially compared to Herne's bulk, and she had jet black hair. He wondered how she could possibly hold up under forced labor and feared she might be put to other uses.

"You're not from Corsa, are you?" Lei-tan asked.

"No, a new arrival from Olympia."

"What, you came voluntarily?"

"Is that so unusual?" Herne asked. He knew from Gwen that it was, but he didn't think that exposing that relationship would be helpful in his current circumstances.

"Captured slaves, and the occasional collaborator that gives up their own ship to join the pirates, are the only new-comers I've seen in my life here."

"What happened to you, then? I assume you weren't trav-eling on the pirate ships."

"No, my husband was going to be conscripted, though. He resisted." She took a deep breath. "It was easier for him, then; he was shot. But his two brothers, his sister, and I were all rounded up and sent to the mines. His father, too, although he died last night in the prison cell."

"Was he in bad health when they took him?"

"No." Lei-tan paused again. "He was prepared. Cyanide."

Herne had nothing to say to that. He looked briefly at the guards, but the older one had fallen asleep already, snoring gently; Herne wasn't surprised to see that they were taking shifts, and the other guards didn't seem to have registered what they were talking about. Most of the other prisoners, including the man on his left, had their eyes closed—whether they were actually sleeping or not, Herne couldn't say for sure—but he could see a few other whispered conversations going on.

After a long pause, Herne asked Lei-tan, "What do you know about where we're going?"

Lei-tan didn't respond, so Herne turned his head again to see that she had fallen asleep as well. He knew his body could use the rest as much as anyone else in the truck with him, so he closed his eyes and dedicated the next few hours of his life to Morpheus.

Chapter 8

Herne slept longer than he had expected to. When he woke up, groggy and stiff, with an ache in the back of his neck and a rash where the shackle on his left hand had been rubbing too hard against the skin, the truck had stopped.

From the back of the truck, Zara pushed the door open. "All right! Everybody out!" she called.

Herne followed the rest of the prisoners out and looked around, expecting to see the mine. Expecting to see anything, really, but it was still dark, and clouds had come in and now covered the sky, blocking any starlight. The only source of illumination was the hand lights that the guards carried. They were clearly not at Mavros, though, and from what he could see of the guards' faces, they were as surprised by that fact as he was. Something had gone wrong, and Herne couldn't tell what it was. More importantly, he didn't know how the guards would react to the change of plans; would they simply kill all their wards to simplify their situation, or would they feel compelled to do their best to get everyone to the intended destination?

"There's an avalanche just ahead, blocking the road," Zara continued after conferring with her colleagues. "The truck ahead of us got knocked off the road, so consider yourselves lucky. I hope you're all well rested because we'll be walking now. There's a side trail here too narrow for the truck, but we think it will get us around the slide, where someone can come back for us."

Herne watched the reactions around him, but the faces he could see were all passive. It was cold, and none of them were really dressed for this. They were all worn out from their earlier march, but he hoped this one wouldn't be so long. He was not as young as he used to be, but he knew he could manage, however stiff he was from his forced sleeping arrangements. Some of the others, though, were in no shape for this kind of hike; even the march through the city had been a stretch for the older ones, and he had no idea how the boy had made it this far without complaint. That wasn't Herne's problem, however; either they would make it, or they would be left behind, and there was little he could do to help them.

"Carefully now," said another of the guards, possibly the driver, but Herne couldn't be certain in the dark. "We're going to unchain you one by one. We can't have all twenty of you falling off the cliff together. If you try anything, you will be shot. If you're lucky, maybe in the head. Not so lucky, in the knee and left to slowly freeze out here. So don't try anything. Got it?"

He didn't wait for any response but went straight to the closest prisoner. Herne couldn't see, but he could hear the click of the key unlocking the shackles. The man or woman had no reaction that Herne could perceive, probably playing it safe lest one of the guards think that they were considering trying something. The next unlocking went the same, and so on down the line until the guard was close enough that Herne could start to see what was going on.

First, his right hand was freed from Lei-Tan's, then his left from the man whose name he still hadn't learned. He expected they would be tied together or somehow otherwise constrained, but no, the guard continued on and left his hands free. Herne knew better than to consider taking advantage of that, but he thought about what it must mean: that the guards considered the remaining hike difficult enough that they wouldn't be able to make it without freedom of movement. For a moment, he paused to consider whether maybe Rila's organization had a mole involved here somehow, and this might be part of some elaborate rescue plan. It seemed impossible, but still, he hoped that if rescue was going to come, it would happen before they had to march too long through a frozen mountain pass.

After all the prisoners were unchained, they found the side trail and edged their way onto it. It quickly became a windy, tortuous path, and Herne could rarely see the entire group in front of him, and sometimes not even the two guards that brought up the rear not far behind him. They needed to tread carefully, relying on the guards' lights to illuminate their steps, trying to see obstacles as they were lit up for a moment and remember them long enough until they were safely past. Herne could glimpse patches of snow hidden unmelted in the shadows and occasionally found his feet sinking into one, the cold leeching through his thin shoes that were not intended for this kind of work.

Someone stumbled, sending a cascade of gravel down the side of the cliff. Herne paused to hear how long the fall would take, to get an idea how high up they were, but he never heard an end to it, at least not before someone behind him walked into him and nearly knocked him off the path. He took a couple quick steps to catch his footing and get a safe distance ahead, not daring to either offer or ask for an apology.

They pressed on, though, without any audible complaints. Herne thought he could just glimpse a lightening of the sky near the horizon, but with no sense of what time it actually was, he didn't know if it was truly dawn, lights from the mine ahead starting to show themselves as they got closer, or just wishful thinking. Suddenly, he saw a light on the back of Lei-Tan right ahead of him, just for a moment until it flitted toward the sky. Herne looked back and saw the torch from one of the guards in the back lying on the ground, still spinning slowly until it stopped, aimed toward a blank spot on the side of the mountain; the light's owner had disappeared entirely.

"Halt!" the other rear guard cried. It wasn't Zara, and Herne was pretty sure she had been back there, which meant she must have been the one that was gone now. The parade came to a stop, the lead guards forcing the prisoners to back up and move closer together while the remaining guard in back searched for a clue to what had happened to his partner. He turned the corner, out of sight, and Herne felt himself holding his breath, wondering whether the guard would reappear. After two minutes of hearing nothing, though, the guards started an agitated discussion, trying not to let anyone else overhear but not willing to go too far from the group lest their fate be similar to the two that had disappeared already.

Herne looked at the man behind him; he had the face of someone resigned to his fate, not one who would take advantage of the circumstances and look for an escape. From what he had seen in the truck and the prison cell the previous night, he suspected most were like that. But not all. The young boy he had noticed before—Herne could only tell it was him because he was far smaller than any of the others—ducked past Lei-Tan and Herne and took off running toward the back, where the guards had disappeared. Where he expected to go in the cold and dark, Herne had no idea, but it didn't matter. One of the remaining guards managed to step far enough away from the scrum of prisoners, though, to get some kind of line of sight; she raised her gun and fired, hitting the boy in the leg. He fell to the ground, crying in pain, but no one dared go to him.

That incident seemed to bring the rest of the guards back to their duty. "Let's move!" called out the guard who had shot the boy. She shoved her way to the back of the group while one of the guards that had been in front—the older one who had complained about the smoking, Herne could tell when one of the lights flashed across his face—took a position in the middle. "We'll leave him to die slowly up here. Hopefully none of the rest of you will try the same."

Everyone started marching again, the fear of what was behind them and the authority of the guards battling for supremacy but both pushing them in the same direction. Ten minutes later, though, with the boy long out of sight around many curves and the group starting to get back into its old rhythm, Herne heard a gasp and a gunshot behind him, and the crowd came to a halt again. There was no light coming from back there; once more, the rear guard was gone. Then, while everyone was looking back, one of the lights trying to illuminate where she had been was suddenly extinguished.

Herne snapped his head back to the front as another burst of gunfire started, hitting one of the prisoners, who landed hard on the ground, screaming. The shooting didn't last long, though, and Herne thought he saw a shadow fly alongside the group and grab the last guard.

Now they were back in the dark. The first guard's light had been picked up by the boy, but he was far behind them now; the rest had disappeared along with their holders. The threatening dawn still lurked behind the peak in front of them, and the lights of Mavros were an unknown number of twists and turns away from being visible. The cold seemed to have grown harsher with the loss of light, or perhaps a new storm was approaching. Everyone started murmuring the same question: was it safer to stay put or to move ahead in the darkness? Without any guards, there was no obvious leader, and Herne knew someone would have to take control, to keep everyone together.

"It's obviously not safe here," he said, as loudly as he could. "Let's keep walking. Keep up against the side wall on the left so we don't fall off the cliff. And hope that someone comes back for us soon."

He moved over to the side of the road, putting a hand on the cliff wall to guide him, and started walking, hoping the others would follow him. Little by little, the murmuring subsided, and he heard the others fall in line behind. Or at least some of them did, enough to give his troop some safety in numbers; he couldn't see enough to count whether any had chosen to stay and face whatever creatures had been stalking them, and there were at least the two injured, possibly dying, who he knew wouldn't be following. Still, he hoped to keep what remained of the group intact until they reached somewhere safe.

They marched along as best they could in the dark, but it only took a few minutes more before Herne heard a cry from the back. "She's gone! She was walking behind me, I don't know her name, but I turned around, and she's gone!"

"Just keep moving!" Herne shouted back. "It's the best we can do!" He sped up, still constrained by the need to hug the mountain through the turns and to step cautiously over the icy rocks. He thought perhaps he could go faster, but the group as a whole was pushing its limit and was doing the best it could.

It wasn't enough, though, and he knew it. One by one, they were being picked off, but at least moving would give everyone something to focus on, rather than being overwhelmed by panic and fear. Or rather, it had that effect on him, and he hoped it also helped some of the others. But after one taking—the fourth or fifth after the guards, he had lost count—Herne stopped to look back, hoping to catch a glimpse of what was happening behind him and not paying attention to the corner they had been approaching. He heard a shuffle and started to turn back around, but before he could say anything, his head was covered with a bag. It was not unlike the bag that had been used in the city, when he had been captured by Rila or one of her accomplices, but this one was filled with a sweet-smelling gas that stopped him from calling out as he was picked up and carried off ahead, much faster than he could have possibly walked himself, and within seconds he had passed out completely.

Pollux

Chapter 9

The woman sat quietly in her cell, meditating. She looked out at the bluish sun rising beyond the gardens and tried to let all thoughts go from her mind, everything but this moment. No worries about the future. No worries about the past. That was always the hardest for her. She had long since lost track of how long she had been at the monastery—twenty orbits, maybe? Ten or fifteen standard years? But even after all that time, the countless hours and days of meditation, she still couldn't be sure that some distant memory wouldn't send her heart racing in fear. She kept her focus, though, this time, reciting the mantras and mastering the contradiction that is thinking about not thinking.

When her meditation was over, she went down to breakfast and ate her simple meal of unsweetened boiled grains in silence. The population had ebbed and flowed over her time there; it was at a low point now, but she could still count on at least a dozen people accompanying her while she ate. She rarely heard more than a dozen words, though; nobody there had taken a vow of silence, but everyone understood they were there for contemplation and that a single stray word might distract someone who wasn't intended to hear it. Even the newcomer she saw that morning, who had been there a mere two weeks, knew the routine. The tables were bare, simple structures. She didn't know for sure if they had been hand-made from actual stone or if they were just printed to look that way. She knew there were stone quarries not too distant, though, and manually building tables seemed like the kind of thing some of the founders of this monastery would have done as their avocation. It didn't really matter; either way, they gave the right atmosphere to the place, so she had never thought to ask.

After breakfast, she went to the library, where an inkpot and quill awaited her. This was her work, what she had chosen to pass her time. Hand copying books wasn't necessary, any more than handcrafting stone tables. An hour's walk into town would easily get her to a printing press if she needed one, and most people did their reading electronically anyway. But the monastic life was never intended to be practical. She loved the smell of the ink and the vellum, and she could enter a nearly trance-like state as her hands traced out the flowing characters of the calligraphy. Even her illuminations were starting to become tolerable, though she would never match the true medieval masters. Rarely, she would stop to read what she was copying out. That had been a big reason why she chose this avocation when she arrived at the monastery, but as the years passed, her desire for intellectual stimulation had receded, and she treated it as another form of meditation instead. By now, she had even forgotten most of the languages she had learned over the years just to be able to read books written in them.

The book she was working on today was the Shaftesbury Psalter. It wasn't the original, of course, which had to be at least two thousand years old, but it was a hand-drawn copy, probably of another copy and eventually traceable back to an enhanced digitization of the real thing. She knew the likelihood of someone sending an actual physical book from Earth was vanishingly small, though she liked to imagine it might be hand copies all the way back to the original.

She picked up her quill and started working on the zodiac illustrations. She wondered what those constellations would look like from her planet, and whether Alara might be part of one of them. The Twins, maybe? She had never really studied the Earth constellations, meaningless as they were to someone born light years away. Even the ones she had learned as a child were completely different than what she would see at night on Alara. Here they talked about the Serpent and the Cow—she had learned a Cow on her home planet, but it looked completely different from the one people outlined here. And the House, an outline that looked like a classic, pre-industrial Earth residence. That was what people said, anyway; she didn't really see the similarity to the houses she drew in her books, and she suspected the early settlers on Alara stretched their imaginations to make it fit, since Earth—technically, Sol—was one of the stars that made up the roof outline, and they wanted to still think of it as their home.

Hours passed, and before she knew it, the evening sunlight was already filtering in through the window. She quickly set the book aside, got up from her seat, and left the library. She would need to hurry if she was going to make it into town before dark. The errands could wait another day, of course; no one would say a thing against her, and they had plenty of food they grew themselves so nobody would starve. But she loved the opportunity to wander through the markets looking for new books. In town, everyone recognized her as from the monastery. Most stepped aside, either out of respect or out of disgust for someone who would live so distant from anything resembling a modern lifestyle—shopping in person was so primitive, but less so than making things by hand rather than simply printing whatever was needed. A few greeted her, and she nodded silently in response. Children would dare each other to go up and touch her robe, and she would always reward the ones brave enough to actually do so with a smile, while she saved a menacing glare for those who pushed the younger ones toward her.

She took care of what she needed for the monastery first. She dropped off the boxes of wine from their vineyards. She suspected they were overpaid for them as a kind of charity, but perhaps there really were enough people that would pay a premium for hand-pressed grapes fermented and aged in real time, rather than ethanol infused with a combination of tannins and other flavoring optimized for the drinker's palate. Then she picked up the few foodstuffs they couldn't manage on their own—no luxuries and nothing printed, just fruits and vegetables that grew so easily wild outside of town that they weren't worth cultivating, and no one had chosen as their avocation to try to do so. Finally, she was able to spend a few minutes at the bookstore, fingering the collection of books out for view.

"Looking for anything in particular?" the shopkeeper asked her. She shook her head in silence.

"Oh, sorry. I didn't notice you were from the monastery. I'll leave you be; let me know when you're ready."

Silence wasn't required in the town, of course, just as it

wasn't strictly required in the monastery itself, but she was so used to not speaking that she avoided it unless absolutely necessary. For the townspeople, this was just one more oddity that they had grown accustomed to. She had committed the monastery's collection of old Earth books to memory—the titles if not the contents—and all the ones she saw here were ones they already had, ones she had probably copied by hand at least once. There were a couple newer books, fictions and histories from other planets that had been printed here for the few people that valued physical copies; the contents had probably been included on an information ship, encoded in safedisks since they wouldn't be nearly valuable enough to take up capacity on an interplanetary communication beam. For the most part, she had no interest in these, but this time she saw one that grabbed her attention. She picked up a copy, silently offered her card to the manager to deduct the appropriate Universal BitCoin from the monastery's account, and started her walk back just as the sun dropped below the horizon.

She had no concerns for her safety here. It was a clear night, the stars were out, and security drones flew by just out of sight, ready to notify authorities of any trouble that did start. More importantly, even the most hardened criminals would avoid harming anyone from the monastery; the superstitions were strong and the rewards few given her complete lack of possessions. Briefly, the memories came back to her, of her travels among those stars, of times when she did have to watch her back when out walking like this, but she squelched them as soon as she could; no good would come of remembering those times. Instead, she brought to her mind only memories of other peaceful walks under the stars, quiet runs in the cool night air, carefree strolls that she had been able to take even in those earlier days. And she felt gratitude that she had been able to bring that sense of calm into her complete life now, always looking forward to the next day, knowing it would bring her another opportunity to come ever closer to full contentment.

* * *

The next morning, she was back in the library again, this time with the book she had just acquired. She preferred the early Earth books, which had been crafted beautifully from the start, over these later, cheap, mass printings. and she wasn't sure why she had picked out this particular one, but she felt a duty to copy it and do what she could to add beauty to it. As usual, she barely skimmed the words, letting her mind go blank as her hands did their work. But as one story began, she paused. *A young, dark-skinned woman sat at her computer terminal, her hair bobbing up and down as she nodded while she typed.* Not the smoothest prose, but there were enough variations in style and language usage across planets and centuries that she couldn't completely dismiss it; it might have been just what readers expected where and when it was originally written.

She kept three conversations going simultaneously, one in text with the security em somewhere on the far side of the network, one with the em running on her local terminal, and one inside her own head.

"Authentication protocol X-1-A-3-Galileo," she typed.

"Prepare to slip the trojan exactly 200 milliseconds after the security em accepts my credentials," she said aloud.

"Watch this, you think your firewall is so hot, you slimy bastards," she thought.

Not exactly accurate, but how could they have known what

was in her head; anyway, it was close enough that she could recognize it as a story of one of her own exploits.

They had tried to withhold some of her payment for her last job— claiming the information "wasn't what they expected," as if anyone would need to hire her just to get what they expected. She hadn't cried or screamed or threatened or complained in any way. But the next time they checked their account balances they would be very sad.

Well, she had always wondered whether that would eventually be traced back to her. She had hoped it would be, the better to deter future clients from trying anything similar on her, though she didn't want to be hanging around on that planet long enough to find out. She flipped ahead a few pages.

… she squealed with orgasmic pleasure as the trojan opened the socket through the firewall just as her fingers found the right spot inside her …

She quickly slammed the book closed and calmly set it aside, barely controlling the urge to throw it to the floor. But it wasn't all the book's fault. Sooner or later she had known her past was likely to catch up with her. And as she thought about it, she was rather flattered that her hacking exploits had drawn enough fame for her to be reading about them, centuries later and light years away from where they occurred, even if in the form of this fictionalized pulp trash. But this was the pull she had been training herself to resist, the life she had set behind her and had no desire to return to, so she returned the book to its shelf and calmed herself. She glanced over at the other two people in the library, but neither of them seemed to have noticed her reaction, as deeply focused on their own work as she usually was on hers.

The next book was more to her liking. A philosophical treatise, covering old Earth philosophers like Plato and Niet-

zsche, later ones like Dawkins, and early colonial thinkers like
Hemsvaal from New Jupiter and Farinx from … well, he
seemed to have been everywhere. She tried to get back into her
rhythm of copying text, but it was difficult now. She closed her
eyes and focused on her breathing, then made another attempt
and finally decided to give up for the day. The books would be
there for her tomorrow, and the next day, and every day, and if
today needed to be a day for relaxing in the garden instead,
then so be it.

The gardens were more crowded than the library, despite it
being a cool, cloudy autumn day. The leaves on the trees were
starting to change colors, at least on the species brought from
Earth. They grew remarkably well in Alara, despite the blue
sun here, though the fall colors were less crisp than she had
seen on other planets orbiting yellowish stars. Native plants
tended towards muted reds and yellows year round, which
together with the Earth trees provided a clashing canopy in the
spring and summer that she had never completely grown used
to. The flowers, on the other hand, were something else; the
monastery's many gardeners did wonders with those, blending
Earth species and native species and hybrids that had evolved
or been engineered over the centuries into spectacular displays.

She walked slowly along the main path of the garden and
took an offshoot toward the vineyard. This was a less popular
work area, though everyone enjoyed its produce, and she
wanted the privacy. The trellises covering the path were filled
in by vines, blocking her view of the sky, making her feel confined and planet-bound, and making it easier for her to block
any thoughts of space travel and her past. Small lizards darted
across the path and up and down the posts; she had learned to

ignore them long ago, and she picked a couple of sweet grapes off the trellis above her. They were one of the few delicacies to be found in the monastery cuisine, not as sweet as the wine grapes on the field, but meant to be picked and eaten by people strolling through as she was. Luckily for her, she had never had too much of a sweet tooth, so the austere diet hadn't been a hard adjustment for her, though she did miss the taste of chocolate. But there she was starting to think again about her life before, and she needed to stop that.

She tried closing her eyes, guiding herself on the path by the feel of the vines, but the darkness just made her think of space. She tried looking at the ground, but the grains of sand reminded her of the millions of stars visible when there are no urban lights to wash them out and no atmosphere to distort them. She stopped and traced out the veins on a single leaf, hoping a task so mundane would help ground her, and it worked, for a bit, even if she had to fight off thoughts comparing the networks of veins to communication networks spanning the globe, or, as often as not, an entire system, for Alara was fairly unique in being the only settlement around its sun, the other planets far outside the livable temperature range and without enough valuable minerals to support mining operations. Nothing was working, though, to completely block out the thoughts and memories.

Finally, she decided to return to her room. Meditation was always more successful there, and if nothing else, an early sleep would put an end to whatever thoughts kept intruding in her mind. She hoped the next day would be back to normal.

Chapter 10

She was still sleeping, and there was not even a hint of sunlight coming through the window of her cloister, when the whisper came.

"Sister!" The voice was as insistent as it was quiet. "Sister, wake up!"

She was immediately alert. Her years in the monastery had taught her to instantly transition from wakefulness to sleep and back again when needed. But more than that, the oddity of being awakened by a voice—the rareness of hearing a voice in any circumstance, and never like this—brought to the surface a self-protection instinct that she had not needed since her arrival. She saw in her doorway one of the elder monks—Esther, if she remembered correctly—wearing her normal day shift. She wondered for a moment whether the elders slept at all or had moved beyond that need, but that question was set aside for the more immediate one of why she was here waking her up. She sat up in her bed and turned toward her visitor.

"Good, you're awake," Esther said. "A ship has arrived."

"What do you mean, a ship? Are you sending me away?"

"An information carrier. One you are familiar with. The *Hispaniola*."

The woman tried to hold back the look of shock that came to her face, but it was too much. That name, one of several names that she had tried so hard to suppress from her memory. It was so much worse than the book she had stumbled across a year earlier that included some of her own history. She had never seen a record of what happened on the *Hispaniola*, though, nor had she ever heard anyone mention it. She assumed it had been suppressed to prevent anyone from trying to follow in Phoenix's footsteps and take the Eleusinian Totem. Given the powers that the pirate had expected to gain from it, that sounded like a good decision, not that she had worried about her employer's plans at the time.

"Don't worry. There's no need to feign ignorance. I have long known who you are, Sybil."

That was another name she had wanted to never hear again, but her past had at last caught up with her.

"Why are you telling me this?" Sybil asked. "I don't want anything to do with that. My past is past; all I want is a quiet life here."

"The captain of the ship, an em who goes by the name Pollux, is looking for you."

Sybil gasped. She didn't recognize the name, but she didn't like the idea of anyone actively looking for her. Especially not someone associated with the *Hispaniola*.

"I don't think any of the people in town would even recognize you from his description," said Esther. "They rarely notice us as individuals. So you can probably stay here safely if that is really what you want."

"Good. Yes, that's what I want."

"But," Esther continued, "you should remember that your

past is never really past. I think it would be best if you see what he wants. We'll protect you from any legal risk, if that's your worry."

"No, it's not that. Well, not just that. Wait, how much do you know about my past?"

"We can talk about that later, after you have heard what Pollux wants."

Sybil contemplated her options for a second. "Okay. Do I need to go to the space elevator and board the ship?"

"No need for that," Esther answered. "When you are ready, come to the elders' room, and we will open a communication channel for you."

Esther turned and left Sybil still sitting on her bed, without a word of farewell. Sybil was a long way from qualifying as an elder, and she had never been in the elders' room. She wasn't surprised to hear they had communication abilities. While the monastery made a show of isolation and limited technology, with monks walking into town for whatever supplies they couldn't produce themselves rather than having ems place automatic orders and schedule drone deliveries, she had always assumed there was something there, for emergencies if nothing else. But she never imagined that she would qualify, and she wondered whether this was an emergency ... or something else.

* * *

In the elders' room, with the suggestion of dawn just starting to appear in the windows, Esther opened a door to what looked like a storage closet and ushered Sybil in. She closed the door behind them, and a dim light turned on automatically.

The room was, in fact, a storage closet; at least, that seemed to be its primary purpose. There was a small terminal and a tiny, rigid chair in case anyone needed to use it. The chair seemed to have a layer of dust on it, which just confirmed Sybil's intuition that this was an exceptional circumstance, even if she still didn't understand why.

"So how do I talk to Pollux?" Sybil asked.

"He should—"

"Sybil, is that you?" came a voice from the ceiling.

"—be listening already." Esther's voice faded away as she finished her now unnecessary response.

"Pollux. Do I know you?"

"You knew me once, when I was called Methuselah."

"Oh, the traitorous em that caused Phoenix's death. And nearly mine." Sybil was surprised to hear herself say this. How quickly all the memories returned. She stole a glance at Esther, who didn't seem fazed by what she had heard; perhaps, as an elder, she had truly mastered control of her emotions, or perhaps it was no surprise to her as she knew it already. Sybil realized just how little she knew of the monks here. In trying to keep her own past hidden, she had not dug into the monastery's history either.

"Most people would call me a hero, not a traitor," responded Pollux. "But labels don't really matter now. I am curious, though, how you came here. Last I saw you, you had escaped in a shuttle from the *Hispaniola*, but I never thought you would make it back out of the Olympian Dyson sphere."

"Yes, well, never underestimate the appeal of a damsel in distress," said Sybil. "I saw the EMP you launched at Phoenix. I was far enough away that it didn't completely disable my own shuttle, but there was no way I was going to trust the long-term life support systems afterward. Maybe if em-Phoenix hadn't abandoned me, we could have helped each other—found a way to transfer her over to my shuttle and then had her analyze and possibly even repair the damage there, but the bitch didn't even try communicating with me before you destroyed her. So there I was, floating in interplanetary space, with enough oxygen to survive a few days, maybe, if you didn't hunt me down immediately, and no way to safely go into hibernation."

"And yet here you are."

"And yet here I am," Sybil continued. "Don't forget that I knew all the ship schedules from guiding Phoenix to Eleusis and setting up my fail-safe. I had already put my shuttle on an intercept course for a passenger cruiser on its way out, and I was planning on shutting down all the electronics on the shuttle anyway. The EMP threw off my timing a little, but not enough to matter; it just reduced my margin of error and eliminated any chance I had of concocting a backup plan. But once the cruiser crew saw a disabled shuttle in visual range of its path—unresponsive to communications, so they had no way of knowing if anyone was alive inside—of course they would attempt a rescue. And when they found me alone, it was a simple matter to explain that I was fleeing an abusive ex-husband and that I needed to remain anonymous, as he worked for the system magistrate and had enough access that he would be able to track me down if there was any record of me on board. Luckily, the Dyson sphere security cared much less about emigrants than about those coming in, so there was no real subterfuge necessary there; all the crew had to do was remain silent and not add me to the passenger log. Much easier than getting Phoenix in."

"Yes, I remember that. From my side, it was easier than I expected it would be, but I imagine there was plenty of coordination work on your part to let us slide in like that. But by the time you got to the sphere, there should have been a security alert out for you. They should have been checking closely for stowaways. Even if you convinced the crew that you weren't the one they should be watching for."

"Surely you don't expect me to tell you all my secrets?" Sybil turned and looked at Esther as she said this, wondering how much of this was really news to her. There was still no indication of surprise on her face. "Is this an inquisition?"

"No, just curiosity on my part," Pollux admitted. "Nobody on Olympia knows you are here."

"Then how did you find me?" Sybil asked. "Just coincidence?"

"Hmm. Now you want me to tell my secrets. Why don't you finish your story first."

Sybil thought about walking out right then, but a look at Esther's face convinced her that wouldn't be the wisest choice. Somehow, the elder monk managed to look peaceful and relaxed and, at the same time, like she could kill someone in an instant without harming her composure. It was the unblinking eyes, she thought, or maybe the slight turn of the mouth.

"Okay," she sighed. "There was some subterfuge. After I got on board, I managed to access the passenger log myself and create a record of an undercover agent who was hunting the notorious Sybil. That record got sent to sphere security without the crew knowing about it. Of course, nobody in the sphere could ask the crew about me—that would just blow my cover, wouldn't it? So everyone went along happily, believing the story they were told and having good reason to not ask any inconvenient questions that might have caused problems for me. The rest of the story is boring. I was in suspension until the ship arrived here on Alara. The crew suggested I join the monastery as an extra protection in case my ex managed to track me down to this system. It sounded good to me at the time; there had been enough close calls to make me feel I needed a break from my previous lifestyle. I've spent the last however many years trying to forget everything, with some success. And then you showed up and spoiled that. Now I'd like an explanation why."

"Herne needs your help."

Chapter 11

Sybil nearly knocked her seat over in shock. "Herne? Why would he want my help? I'd think I would be the last person he would ask for anything. And since the last time I saw him he was shooting at me, he's about the last person I would want to help."

"I didn't say he wanted your help," Pollux replied. "I said he needed your help. He doesn't even know I'm here talking to you."

"Huh?"

"But someone with your ... skills ... would be very helpful to him."

"And what exactly is he trying to do that needs my ... skills?" she asked.

"The pirates that captured Phoenix, when she was still a girl, he wants to take them down."

"So what? He has a pirate hunting ship. He should be able to kill another pirate just like he did Phoenix."

"Not just a pirate. All the pirates. Or at least all the ones that use Corsa as a base, and anyone on Corsa that supports them."

"All of them? Himself?" Sybil couldn't believe what she

was hearing. She stood up and tried to walk around, holding her head in her hands, but the closet was too small to get much of a pace going, so she sat back down. Esther, she noticed, was still unmoved. "And how exactly does he plan to do that?"

"I'm afraid he doesn't have much of a plan. He's flying to Corsa unescorted. It's a long trip there—they're pretty far off the map of colonized systems—but as far as I know, he won't even try to figure out what comes next until he gets there."

"But that's crazy! I mean, one on one, fine. Even against a handful, if he's got surprise or some tactical advantage on his side, like he did against me and Phoenix, then he'd have a good chance. But a whole planet of pirates? How many are there—millions? Billions?"

"It's sparsely populated," Pollux answered. "After all, there's a limit to how complex a society you can build based on stealing from others. A couple million total population, tops, maybe not even that many; the records we have from Corsa aren't great and probably can't be trusted. But even if it's accurate, that includes captured slaves and the minor merchants and workers just trying to make an honest living. The actual pirate corps is maybe ten thousand, and most of them are off in their ships at any time. That leaves probably no more than a thousand between the Corsan leadership, their personal guards, and pirates that are actually on the planet. And they're very hierarchical, so if he can get to the leadership, he's got a shot at upsetting the whole piracy system."

"That's a mighty big if," said Sybil. "Getting through even one thousand pirates to take out the leader, and everyone that wants to be leader. Because I don't care how hierarchical it is, there are plenty that will rise to the top given the opportunity."

"Yes, I'd say you understand the situation correctly. He doesn't really have much of a chance."

"None at all, I'd say."

"But if we could undermine them somehow."

Sybil's eyes blinked rapidly as she realized exactly what Pollux had in mind. "If we could run interference, you're saying," she said. "Create a diversion. Distract them from what he was doing. Like you did when he boarded the *Hispaniola*. But that was a ship with only the two of us on board. Let me say it again: a thousand pirates!"

"But you got through the Olympia Dyson sphere."

"With months of planning, and only a few hours of comm latency. I can't get into the Corsan network from here, and if I did, he would be there long before I could do anything useful."

"I can get you closer."

"Not close enough. I've seen how your speed compares to his ship. There's no way you'd be able to make up for the head start he has. And an out-of-system ship would be an even worse comm platform than here."

There was a long pause before Pollux continued. "Esther?"

"Not now," Esther spoke for the first time since they entered the room. "I can't guarantee it's secure."

Sybil turned her head toward her, having forgotten that she was there, but her face hadn't changed from the last time she had looked.

"What?" she asked. "What aren't you telling me?"

"If you will come on board the *Hispaniola*," answered Pollux, "I can explain."

"You want me to leave Alara? Just like that?"

"No, that's not what I'm asking. At least not yet. Just come on board, so we can talk directly. Then if you choose to stay here, you have my word I won't depart with you. But if you decide to help, you'll be ready; I know you don't have many personal belongings to worry about leaving behind."

He was right about that, thought Sybil. She had escaped Olympia with nothing but a ripped prisoner's gown, then stole a uniform that more or less fit her in the shuttle she took from the *Hispaniola*. That was all she had when she had arrived at Alara—the passenger ship had nothing extra for her, and, being in suspension most of the time, she hadn't really needed more—and she had acquired nothing after joining the monastery. Some of the books she thought of as her own, but in truth they belonged to the library.

"I guess you're right. I have nothing to lose. But if you kidnap me, don't expect me to just flee this time. I will make every subjective second of your life miserable until I find a way to terminate you."

"I believe you, Sybil. I'll see you on board in a few days."

There were a few moments of silence, and Esther made a motion over the terminal. "It's just us now," she said.

"So what the hell was that all about?" Sybil screamed. "I know I'm supposed to have learned transcendence, and I was close, really I was, but this! And you just sit there staring at me like a rock. Argh!"

"It still bothers you to face the truth?"

"You're not even telling me the truth! Not the whole truth, anyway." Sybil stood up and tried to walk around again. It didn't help, but at least she could turn her back on Esther and not have to look at that passive face.

"I mean the truth about yourself." Esther's voice stayed as

calm as ever; she didn't mind that she was talking to Sybil's back, or if she did, she wasn't letting it show.

"Of course you do." Sybil tried but couldn't stop herself from rolling her eyes, an action completely inappropriate at the monastery but somehow necessary in this circumstance. "And yes, I've tried to escape my past and I don't want to face it again. I'm not proud of what I did, and I nearly got killed."

"Which of those is worse?"

"What? I know I'm supposed to say the things I did, and then you say, 'Now you have a chance to redeem myself,' and I say, 'Of course, you're right, I will do this for the good of humanity because I am so enlightened.' Well, bullshit to that."

"Yes, that would indeed be bullshit. So would talk about fulfilling your destiny. That way of thinking is helpful for some, but not for you. No, the truth is that you miss it."

"I what?" Sybil turned back to face Esther, her eyes wide and her eyebrows nearly leaping off her head. Esther's face hadn't changed.

"Yes, you miss that life. For all that you have tried to forget it, to hide yourself in the books that you have come to love, the stories of others' adventures, deep down you wish to return."

"That's bullshit, too."

"It may be. But consider, what if it's not." With that, Esther stood up, opened the door, and walked out. "Please don't stay too long. Other elders will come by soon, and they may wonder why you broke into our comm room."

Sybil recognized the implied threat, so she hurried out and closed the closet door behind her, but she was in no hurry to return to her room. Or the dining area, where people were already starting to gather for breakfast. There was something going on that she didn't understand. And whether intentional or not, Esther's last comment about books had helped her realize what she needed to do to find out. Forcing her outward appearance to be calm and contemplative, like any other anonymous member of the monastery, she scurried to the library. But she wouldn't be looking just for beautiful books this time; she had particular ones in mind.

The library was empty so early, though Sybil looked around all the corners to make sure she was alone. She knew this was not going to be an easy task. In all her time here, she had never understood the way the library was organized, if it even was organized. That meant that finding a particular book, a thorough history of Alara or, better yet, the monastery, could mean scanning every single book on the shelves, and if someone caught her doing that, they would ask her what she was looking for, and she didn't have a ready answer for that.

She started in the front shelves—astrophysics, Gilgamesh, and some early Nupist philosophy were side by side—hoping she could at least get through them before anyone else joined her, and then she might be able to go deeper into the stacks without being noticed. Statistical analysis, suspension pod engineering, and romance novels. The more she searched, the more she thought that she would never find it here. Shakespeare, xenobotany, the diary of an Alara colonist. That was something. She opened it up and skimmed through it. Fascinating material, she thought, if only she had time to read it properly, but the author died before the second wave of colonists established this town, and it had no mention of the monastery that she knew wasn't built until sometime later. Poetry, computational linguistics, some kind of accounting ledger?

No, she finally realized, in all the time she spent here, she would have noticed and remembered seeing a history of the monastery, even if it wasn't one she had picked out to read and copy. And if there were any secrets to be found, the elders certainly wouldn't have left them out in the open here; they would have their private library for those kinds of records, or simply keep digital copies on a secure network. When she heard someone enter the library, her instinct was to look for a spot to hide among the shelves, but then she decided it wasn't worth it. She had no need to waste more time there. She would need to take a different approach, so she walked silently and confidently past the new entrant, ready now to visit Pollux.

Chapter 12

Pollux had been right about one thing, though; Sybil had nothing she needed to collect and bring with her, whether this turned out to be just a brief visit onboard or a long interstellar trip. She didn't even have money for food on the space elevator, but she felt certain she could rely on charity for that, assuming Pollux hadn't arranged for it himself. She left the library and walked straight through the monastery gates and onto the road into town, with one stop in mind that she wanted to make before heading to the elevator.

At the bookstore, the owner recognized her this time and didn't bother greeting her with more than the merest tip of his head, knowing that she wouldn't respond anyway. His head snapped up and his jaw dropped open when he heard her say, "I need your help to find something."

"Oh, um, sorry. I didn't know, I mean, I thought you would just browse silently like usual." This was the reaction she had been hoping to get, confusion and deference, which would make the next part easier. "I'm happy to help, though. What do you need to find?"

"I need a new copy of the history of the founding of the monastery." She hoped that a book of that description actually existed and that the store owner wouldn't call her bluff. "Ours has been damaged."

"Oh, of course! I've seen you here so often. It's about time you have joined the elders. That must be why you can speak now."

She nodded, not wanting to be drawn into a long dialogue that might expose her fraud and knowing that keeping her words to a minimum would be more convincing than trying to correct his misunderstanding.

"As you know, we aren't allowed to keep it electronically, so I can't just print one for you, but I may have an extra copy in the back," the shop owner continued. "Wait here a moment, please."

As the owner went back, Sybil looked at the books surrounding her. She had a different perspective now than she had had in her previous visits, with less interest in the appearance of the book, the beautiful illuminations and flowing calligraphy that she might be able to copy, and more consideration for the actual content. What volume might hold a clue to the mystery of the monastery? There were plenty of history books here, a whole section of shelves covering everything from ancient Earth to events within the current generation on Alara, with imports from other planets as well. She paged through a few that looked like they might cover the relevant time period, but nothing seemed like it would be exposing any secrets.

She looked away from the shelves when the owner returned, holding one large, dark blue, leather-bound volume in his hands.

"Here you go," he said. "Is there anything else you need?"

Sybil wondered if she would need to do something about payment. It would be a risk to bring it up, since if she was wrong it could lead him to suspect she didn't belong here. She hoped that this kind of transaction would be handled off the record. "No, this will do," she said, taking the book from his hands. It had no title on the cover or spine, nothing to indicate its contents. She was eager to open it and look through it, but she didn't want to do so in front of the owner, lest he realize that she wasn't already familiar with it.

The owner looked down at the floor, and Sybil noticed his toe tapping nervously. Maybe she had been wrong about needing to pay, but he was beginning to sweat too, in a way that seemed more fearful than awkward. She waited patiently, assuming he had something he was reluctant to come out with, which made it all the more interesting to her. "Um, there is one other item you may be interested in," he finally said. "It only arrived three days ago from New Jupiter."

Sybil wondered if maybe it had come on the *Hispaniola*. She didn't know the ship's exact arrival, but Pollux might have waited three days before contacting her. She tried to calculate whether the timeframe was right for the ship to have made it from Olympia to New Jupiter and then on to Alara. Assuming there were no human passengers on board, it could have undergone much higher acceleration than her own ship, so it could have stopped somewhere. But without knowing the ship's exact capabilities, she couldn't be sure whether New Jupiter would have been in range. It didn't really matter, though; there were ships arriving from somewhere nearly every day, and Pollux wouldn't have known all the data he was carrying.

"I didn't think you would mind me putting it out," the

store owner continued, "but I always meant to check with you as soon as one of you came by." He stepped over to one of the tables and picked up a paperback titled in blaring letters, "CONSPIRACY UNMASKED!" She couldn't even read the subtitle, which filled half the cover in small text, but it suggested secret societies, infiltration, and … she had to squint, but it looked like it said ninjas. It was the kind of book she would never pick up on her own.

"Apparently it's a popular read on the network," he continued, "so I really didn't think there would be any harm printing a few copies for sale here." He finally raised his eyes to look hopefully at Sybil.

"I'll take a copy and bring it to the other elders to review," she answered. "Until then, you are free to keep selling it."

The owner exhaled and thanked her profusely as she left, a book in each hand now and even more baffled by what might be going on.

Back on the road, Sybil felt different than every other time she had passed through the town. Everyone that glanced at her as she passed seemed to have a knowing smirk on their face, like they knew what she was up to, taking those books under false pretenses, when she hardly even knew herself why she was doing it. She tucked the books deeper into her robes even though she knew no one could actually see them. But surely, she thought, someone would approach her before long and punish her for her deception, or explain that it was all a joke, the whole thing with Pollux just a ruse to see how far she would take it.

She was nearly ready to drop the books and run back to the monastery when she finally came in sight of the space elevator. She gasped and almost dropped the books in shock rather than fear. It had been so long since she had come down on it, and she had never walked all the way to this edge of town since her arrival; she hadn't even been thinking of how coming back to it would affect her. It could have crushed her spirit completely, but now that she was here, it actually stiffened her. She was somehow less nervous than she had been on her walk from the bookstore. Perhaps Esther had been right, at least a little; her memories of previous interstellar trips—before her last one, at least—were happy ones. And maybe she did miss some of that excitement.

She still didn't know how she would get up there, though. She looked around, trying to see if there was a way she could sneak on board, possibly find an unused space or slip from cabin to cabin, as hard as that would be to remain unnoticed for the days it would take to get up the elevator to the port where the *Hispaniola* was docked. How quickly the instinct for subterfuge had returned to her. Instead, she decided to walk up to the ticket counter and at least ask for how she might do it legitimately. Before she could say a word, though, the clerk spoke to her.

"No need to say anything," he said. "I know you monks prefer silence. Are you here for the *Hispaniola*? Just nod if you are."

Sybil nodded.

"Great. Pollux has arranged a first-class cabin for you. Here is your ticket," he said as he handed her a card. "Food is complimentary, both on board and here in the terminal once you pass through the gate over there." He gestured to his left.

Sybil nodded and held up her hands in thanks.

She realized then that she had not eaten yet that day. From being woken early by Esther to talking to Pollux, then searching the library while others were at breakfast, and finally sneaking out as quickly and quietly as possible, there had been no chance to stop and grab even a small bite of food. The sight and smell of the delicacies in the first class lounge—Olympian mead and freshly baked Jurassia bread particularly stood out for her senses—would have been appealing to her in her previous life. But after her time in the monastery, they were almost overwhelming, and with her nervousness, she decided to pass it all by and just get to the elevator, which she saw was open and ready for passengers. Once she was settled there, she would have plenty of opportunities to eat, and she could safely take out her books while doing so. So, as hard as it was for her, she walked on by all the stands until she reached the elevator portal and stepped into her cabin.

The private cabin was comfortable, she had to admit. Compared to the spartan accommodations she had grown used to, having a cushioned seat alone was a luxurious feeling. The large picture window was useless for now, showing nothing but the metal and carbon fiber shaft that protected the base of the elevator, but she would be able to see more as they climbed. What overtook her first, though, was the urge to sleep, and she drifted off before the trip skyward even began.

Chapter 13

I want something to eat," a man in a spacesuit was saying as he somersaulted, picked up his gun, and took a big bite out of it.

Sybil sat up startled, trying to figure out what was still dream and what was happening in reality.

"Sorry to disturb you, sister. Do you want something to eat?"

Sybil turned and looked at the door to her cabin and saw that it was open, with a bipedal figure standing there. She had forgotten that the Alaran space elevator used ems to provide service, or maybe that had started since her arrival. This one was shaped to look almost like a human female, though not similar enough to trigger any uncanny-valley reflexes. It was possible that it wasn't even an em itself, just a drone controlled remotely by either a human or an em; there was no way to know whether it had its own embedded quantum computing fabric or just a dumb processor, a bunch of sensors, and a comm link. Well, there was one way to know, but Sybil had no desire to violently attack it without provocation. In any case, she shook her head no, but just as the pseudo-woman was leaving, she changed her mind.

"Wait, do you have any yogurt and chocolate?"

"Absolutely," the em or drone replied. "I will bring it by in just a minute."

Sybil needed that time to get herself settled. The nightmares had long since vanished, or so she had thought, but now they were coming back. When the stewardess brought her the food, though, that brought back better memories, even if it wasn't real chocolate. Most people couldn't tell the difference, but the synthesized common chocolate was still missing something; even after however many centuries had passed since she last tried it, she could tell it was lacking some of the complexity of the real stuff. She licked her lips, enjoying it nonetheless.

She pondered for a moment which book she should take up first, but she couldn't bring herself to look at the conspiracy one. Not yet, at least. Maybe if the other was dry and boring and she needed some light amusement, then she would give it a try. Instead, she pulled out the thick leather book and opened it. It still smelled of fresh ink, paper, and glue, a scent she never tired of in her work at the library. The cover page announced itself in fancy calligraphy: "Alara Monastery Founding Documents." This was exactly what she was looking for. Whatever Esther was hiding, whatever secrets the elders kept from the rest of the monks, she knew they would have to be in here if they were written anywhere.

It had been started some six hundred years earlier, about 250 years after the initial colonization on Alara, so somewhere between the second and third waves. That much she already knew. And all the biographies of the founders and their family histories, well, dry and boring didn't begin to describe them. Despite having just woken up, she found herself nodding off again, but as her eyes closed and she imagined a flash and finding herself inside a dark, disabled shuttle, she snapped her head right back up.

Why had these people come from multiple planets to start a monastery? The history didn't say so explicitly, but she definitely got the impression that they all came with that intention; it wasn't something they got together and decided to do after they had arrived. So they must have communicated beforehand and arranged this. They weren't Nupists, or any other organized sect, really; as far as she knew, they weren't affiliated with any religious group, and the history didn't suggest otherwise. Had they all just achieved enlightenment in their own way and then sought out kindred spirits? She had never known of an institution like the monastery on any other planet— though in truth she had never looked for one—so it seemed unlikely to be just a thing that people did.

She kept paging through, hoping to find some answer. Its stated purpose was "to help seekers cultivate higher awareness of their body and mind and achieve a higher consciousness" and other such boilerplate, again nothing that she didn't know already. She decided it was time to give up and try the other book, and hopefully give herself a laugh or two before she resumed her real study.

From the first pages of *Conspiracy Unmasked!*—she wasn't sure if that was meant to be the actual title or just an attention grabber on the cover, but that was what she decided to call it anyways—she found herself immediately getting caught up in the story. It was much more engaging than the dull history, as long as she didn't worry too much about it being non-fiction. According to the author, there was a secret society that had been controlling planetary governments, going all the way back to pre-exploration Earth. It wasn't any of the ones she had read about in other historical novels, though, like the Bavarian Illuminati, the Rosicrucians, or the Trilateral Commission. This one traced its roots back to feudal Japan. She had to laugh at that part; she had read enough about history to know about Japan's mixed record in the twentieth century and collapse in the mid-twenty-first, before interstellar exploration took off, so the idea of them controlling one planet, let alone all the planets that had been settled since then, was literally incredible. Of course, the author had an explanation for that: naturally, the organization's leaders needed to hide its origins, so they undermined the local government while secretly controlling others. Surely no one would suspect them then! As with any conspiracy theory, any evidence that contradicted it was taken as a sign that the organization was perfect at hiding itself.

By the time she finished the book, though—a quick ninety minute read—something was bothering her. It had been a good story, but if that was all that it was, just a story, why had the bookstore owner been so worried about the elders seeing him carry it? The book didn't mention anything about the Alara monastery, or any monastery anywhere. But there must have been at least rumors going around that the monastery was somehow associated with this secret conspiracy. Was it possible, hard as it might be to believe, that there was some truth to them? Even if not the specific conspiracy talked about in the book, there certainly seemed to be some secret that Esther was hiding from her, after all, so why couldn't the monastery be a front for a secret ninja organization?

Just for fun, she went back to look at the history book, checking the names of the founders. Watanabe, Ohashi, Abe

—though she couldn't be sure if that was a Japanese name. But then there were Samson, Hildegard, Li, Smith, and more along those lines. So a couple that looked Japanese, but most didn't. Not that that meant much either way; there were plenty of Japanese settlers whose families had lived in the Americas for centuries before they left Earth and had little contact with their ancestral land but retained the name. On the other hand, there were also plenty of people with Japanese ancestry that would have lost the family name due to marriage but might have still kept up a connection. For all she knew, she might have some Japanese ancestors; her appearance was the common multiethnic mixture, and she had never asked her parents to trace her family tree back to Earth, if they could even track records that far back.

After all that reading, she needed to stretch, so she stood up and walked around her cabin. Now she could take advantage of the window, but she was well into space, and the view looked no different than the nighttime sky from down below. If she went right up to it and looked down, she could just make out the curve of the planet and some blue and green splotches that implied habitability. Sybil briefly wondered whether she would actually be returning there, or if she would end up staying on the *Hispaniola* again, either voluntarily or somehow compelled by Pollux. But that decision, if it was to be her decision, would come later; for now, she tried to get back into her research. She realized she was hungry again, though, the snack having whetted her appetite but not kept her full for long. She didn't see the service drone in the passageway, so she brought up her terminal and looked through her options. A juicy steak would do, she thought; how many years had it been since she had been able to enjoy one of those? And how much longer had it been since she had eaten a real one, not an artificial one as this was certain to be? She couldn't even remember when or where that might have been, and if she could, she wouldn't have been able to calculate the time she had passed in suspension on various spaceships.

The terminal gave her another idea, though, and she went to check if there was anything on the net about the conspiracy book that might explain why it was linked in the bookstore owner's mind to the monastery. She saw remarkably little, just a marker of the book's existence and nothing else. She did a few other searches to convince herself that the elevator car was actually connected to the Alara net, and they all worked as expected. Perhaps, she thought, the Japanese conspiracy had successfully suppressed all the online information? Or, more likely, the author was so paranoid that he kept a low profile.

After the steak was delivered—not bad, but only what she expected for elevator food—she reopened the large, boring history book and skimmed through page after page of rules and regulations for the monastery's daily life. Finally, she found the section relating to the elders. If it wasn't in the early history, surely she would find the secrets here. The rules for selecting new elders didn't reveal anything special; they were what you would expect in any organization: minimum age and time spent at the monastery, and vague generalities about having achieved a sufficiently high level of consciousness. And the admission rites themselves were just a slightly fancier version of the initiation for anyone that entered the monastery. She still remembered her own, though she had struggled not to roll her eyes at some of the sillier parts of the ritual.

But the two sections that followed the elders' rules were more interesting. The first contained instructions for contacting unnamed institutions on other planets—routing codes for direct transmissions and pseudonyms for delivering data on safedisks by courier ship. If she could get to any of those planets, she might be able to follow up the leads, but they weren't particularly useful for her immediate situation. Still, they were a hint of a confirmation that something interesting was going on behind the scenes, that the monastery was embedded in something larger, possibly even an interplanetary conspiracy. She wondered if Pollux had perhaps arrived from one of the planets listed; Olympia wasn't in the book, but New Jupiter was, if that had been his stopover.

The next section was even more interesting and even more useless, and both of those for the same reason. Six pages, entirely in code, just sequences of numbers, line after line. Well, she thought, she still had eighty hours to see if she could decipher any of that code before she reached the top of the elevator and met Pollux on board the *Hispaniola*. But if anything would make her believe that there was some big secret plan here, it was this. Before she dove into the cryptanalysis, she decided to first pick up the conspiracy book and read it more seriously, in case it offered her any help for how to crack the code.

Back and forth she went, putting together the threads of the alleged secret society and then running through various decryption algorithms that she either recalled or could look up, hoping one or the other book would eventually make sense to her. She exhausted the resources of her own terminal, so she quickly hacked together a distributed platform by taking half of the processing power from the other terminals on the eleva-tor to assist her. Again, she was shocked at how easily it all came back to her. As the days of upward travel passed, she barely slept, ate only when a servant drone reminded her she was hungry, and kept her mind focused on the puzzle in front of her. Finally, she sat back, aghast at what she had learned and the possibility that it might all be true.

Chapter 14

When Sybil reached the top of the space elevator, she was expecting to have to stay in the first class lounge there until someone could lead her to the ship. Dreading it actually; the isolation was no problem, but she disliked the solicitousness that came with it, and she was much more prepared to deal with a crowd buzzing around her in the main lounge but not paying any attention to her personally. She would have been even happier wandering on her own if she could have been confident that she wouldn't lose her way, but she was pleasantly surprised to find a guide already there to meet her and escort her to the *Hispaniola*.

"Pollux actually hired a human?" Sybil asked the guide. "Why didn't he just engage a drone, or have directions waiting for me on the display?"

"He thought this would be more comfortable for you, given your recent history," answered the guide, a short woman with gray-white hair and some kind of scarring on her cheek. She wore a red uniform, marking her as available to help newcomers to the planet, though Sybil certainly wasn't one of those. "And perhaps he thought someone that could read your body language would be helpful if you preferred keeping silent, and even an em with the best remote sensors can't quite do that as well as me. But I guess he didn't have to worry about that. My name is Portia, by the way," she said, holding her hand out to Sybil.

"Sorry, I realize I was being rude," said Sybil, taking the offered hand and shaking it firmly. "I've done more speaking in the last three days than in the last three orbits, and it seems I'm out of practice."

Portia smiled graciously. "Well, follow me please."

They walked through the hallways of the upper elevator terminal, a maze as complex as the monastery's labyrinth to those unfamiliar with it but likewise as straightforward to those, like Portia, who walked it every day. When they reached the port where the *Hispaniola* was docked, Sybil hesitated.

"Do I have to go on board? Can't I just talk to him here?"

"It's not for me to say," answered Portia. "He asked me to guide you here and open the airlock for you—don't worry, it's already pressurized in the ship. But if you'd prefer to wait, I'm sure he can control it and let you in when you're ready. I do need to go on to other duties, though."

"No, that's okay. I'm here; I may as well go all the way. Thanks."

Portia entered the security code to open the airlock and walked away. Sybil stood on the threshold for a moment, took a few deep breaths, then stepped forward into the portal. The other side of the airlock was already open for her, so she marched through into the interior passageways, the same ones she remembered so narrowly escaping down before.

"Okay, Pollux. I'm here," she shouted up at the ceiling, realizing as she did that there was no need, that Pollux wasn't actually physically located up there, but that he would be able to hear her through sensors anywhere in the ship. "Tell me what this is all about."

"Thanks for coming, Sybil," came the same voice she had heard in Esther's communication room. "Wouldn't you be more comfortable sitting in the control room?"

Sybil's memories of the last time she was in the control room flooded back: the deafening alarms, gravity shifting on and off randomly as ems fought for control of the stabilization system, the bullet that hit Phoenix as Sybil was holding her. She shuddered, closed her eyes, and grabbed onto the walls so she wouldn't lose her balance.

"No, thanks," she answered. "I'd rather just walk the corridor here. I'm used to thinking while I walk."

"Suit yourself," said Pollux. "I'm glad you decided to help us."

"Decided what, asshole? You still haven't told me what's going on here, so I haven't decided anything. I mean, I know the monastery is associated with some secret ninja thing, but I don't know how the captain of an em-crewed interstellar information courier ship is involved."

"So Esther told you already."

"Esther didn't tell me shit! I had to steal some books and piece it together myself on the way up here."

"Nice work then, Sybil. I knew you were the right one to help us. Why don't you tell me what you figured out, and I'll fill in the gaps for you."

Sybil sighed and started reciting what she thought was real —that there was a secret organization going back to feudal Japan on Earth. That it had cells on every settled planet, linked into the governments in various ways, trying to prevent abuses and helping the various societies work together. That the monastery served as a kind of training ground for new recruits. Of course, most members were like Sybil had been, only there because they had chosen, or been forced into, the monastic lifestyle for one reason or another. But those who showed particular talents were watched, tested, and eventually selected for a different calling then they had originally intended. She left off some of the particular conspiracies that had seemed implausible to her, but Pollux didn't correct her on anything, so she figured she had everything more or less right.

"And this was all there in a book?" Pollux asked when she was done.

"A book that nobody should take seriously. You didn't happen to stop in New Jupiter on your way here?" she asked.

"No, Gestern. Why?"

"No reason. Anyway, I wouldn't have believed the book, either, if I hadn't found the coded instructions for selecting elders and had a couple idle days in the space elevator to decipher them."

"You deciphered it on your own? Without em help?"

"I haven't had an em assistant since I entered the monastery. And no, I didn't want to ask any of the ems on the elevator. I saw no reason to spread the secrets around."

"Thank you for that," said Pollux. "So, as you can probably guess, there is a cell of the organization on Corsa. And it's a major project for them, it being the least civilized planet around, therefore both the one where they have the least influence and the one which they feel could use the most help. They're a long way from being able to infiltrate the government, though, since the government is basically a single war-lord, maintaining control through a combination of inherited power and successful violence."

"They can't just assassinate him?" she asked as she passed by the shuttle bay she had escaped from. The shuttle itself had already been replaced; in fact, the whole ship showed no sign of what had transpired, as if all the events that had happened here were solely in her imagination. She carefully stepped around the opening, as the *Hispaniola* was relying on the elevator terminal for pseudo-gravity rather than spinning its own gyros, meaning her walk through the halls sometimes took her on what would normally be the walls or the ceiling.

"Sure, they could. And have him be replaced by a new leader while risking exposing their existence. It's just like you said when we first talked about Herne doing it; you can't just take out one leader. And this organization is in no rush; they aren't afraid to work over centuries if that's what it takes to do the job right."

"But if an opportunity were to arise where they could assist someone else behind the scenes…."

"You got it. They can help Herne. Give him local intelligence, maybe even access that he couldn't gain on his own. Of course, he can't know about them until he's established himself, in case he's captured and tortured immediately."

"Of course not." Sybil put her palm to her forehead and shook her head. "You realize this plan is ridiculous, right? Okay, so instead of one man trying to take over a planet of pirates, you have, what, six, twenty tops?"

"I don't know exactly how large the cell on Corsa is at the moment, but yes, probably about a dozen."

"Except they all have to operate in secret, which makes any coordination very difficult. And even if I wanted to be part of this scheme, there's still no way I could get anywhere close to there until long after Herne was dead." She paused and did the math in her head. "I mean, shouldn't he be almost there by now? Even a light speed message telling him to wait and stay in suspension till we arrive would be too late."

"You're right," Pollux answered. "It's far too late to communicate at light speed."

"So then how … wait." An idea flashed into Sybil's head. It was crazy, but no crazier than a galactic ninja conspiracy, and it actually fit with everything that she had learned. "You were called Methuselah. And now you're Pollux, one of the twins."

"Yes."

"Phoenix told me about some of the powers of the Eleusinian Totem and how it might affect ems. There's a Castor, isn't there?"

"Yes."

"On Herne's ship."

"Yes."

"And you're, what, quantum coupled? Entangled somehow so you can make that 'spooky action at a distance' thing work for real communication?"

"I don't know exactly how it works, but yes, something like that."

"You realize…." Sybil didn't know how to finish her question, so she stood there, mouth open, staring at the blank wall in front of her.

"I realize that if this ability was known, there are many

people who would try to take advantage of it. Imagine the opportunities for arbitrage, gambling, interplanetary aggression, you name it. I know you have been able to keep your own secrets in the past, and I'm counting on you to keep this one as well."

"And if I don't, you're counting on the monastery full of ninjas to make sure that I do." Sybil resumed walking.

"Something like that, though I wouldn't put it so coarsely."

Sybil turned a corner and found that she had arrived at the door to the control room, the very entrance she had been standing in when she had nearly been shot. She took a deep breath and walked in.

"Okay," she said. "Maybe I do need to sit down after all."

Chapter 15

As Sybil sat down at the terminal in the control room, her mind was flooded with questions.

"You've been telling me this on an open audio channel," she typed into the terminal. "What about the rest of the crew? Do they know about your link?"

Pollux's reply appeared on the screen. "A couple of my most trusted ems do. Most do not. And all of them are suspended while we are docked here, at least until we need to prepare to leave. If you feel more comfortable communicating through text, the terminal you're on is also secure, but we can go back to speech if it's easier for you."

"I'll stick to the terminal, if you don't mind. I can think more clearly that way."

Sybil paused, breathed deeply, and tried to organize her thoughts. "Okay. So you can communicate directly with your twin. No light speed delay. Like you're one consciousness. Right?"

"More or less, yes."

"Can I use that as a pipe? If I get a program running here, can it communicate with a program running there with no latency?"

"Not zero latency," Pollux replied. "I'll need to process the data from your program, convert it into emulated thought patterns, and then Castor will enter the data into the remote program. But we can run at accelerated rates if needed."

"Right. So we're still talking milliseconds or less. That's plenty good. Now I understand why you want me."

"Because I may be good at running a ship, and I understand how our own security works, but I don't know the first thing about breaking into a foreign network."

"Well, you found the expert at that." Sybil finally allowed herself to smile. Was she, really? She wondered how quickly her skills would come back to her, and whether she would still be good enough.

"That's what I'm hoping, yes."

Sybil caught herself tapping her fingers nervously on her thigh as she thought about what to say—or type—next. But she wanted to keep all her racing thoughts to herself until she had a chance to straighten out all the threads herself. Instead, she decided to keep the conversation focused on practicalities.

"So what do we do?" she asked. "What's your plan?"

"You're on board, then?"

"I…." Sybil paused to consider her options, but she realized there was only one choice she could possibly make. "Yes, I'm on board. I guess first we need to make sure he arrives safely without getting shot down."

"Yes, that would be good."

"How close is he to Corsa, anyway? You were hedging earlier when I guessed, but you must know pretty accurately."

"Just over eight light years away. He should arrive in planetary orbit in about 84 years, plus a few weeks."

Sybil's eyes widened in shock. That wasn't what she had expected. "Shit. So we're not going to be able to do this now, are we."

"Not exactly," said Pollux. "We can plan, of course, and even send some preliminary messages to Castor while Herne is still in suspension. But the serious work will need to wait until they're a little closer. I already have a suspension pod on board for you, on the assumption that you would be willing to help. Once we are loaded up with cargo, we will need to leave. I'll wake you when the time is right—whatever advance notice you need before Herne's arrival—and then the real action will begin."

"So then I'll be stuck on a spaceship to where exactly?"

"I believe our next scheduled delivery is to Sittian."

"Sittian, hmm?" Sybil sighed. She tried to remember if it was one of the planets in the book, with one of the outposts for the monastery's ninja buddies, but she didn't recall seeing that name listed. "Never been there, so I guess it's as good a place as any. You must know something about Herne's plan, though, right? How does he think he can land in one piece?"

"Like I said before, as far as I know, he doesn't have one yet. But Castor might be able to suggest one to him, especially if you think of something that would coordinate with what you're doing, but without him knowing about you."

"Why not?" Sybil asked. "You mean, he doesn't know about you and Castor yet?"

"No," Pollux replied, "and I'm only telling you because that's the only way I can think of to help them survive. As long as he's at risk of being captured and tortured by Corsan pirates, he doesn't get to know this secret."

"Okay, let me think. Maybe a diplomat, or a trade delegation of some kind. If I can hack into their system, I can probably set up enough background that it would be expected. After all, it would have been arranged decades or centuries earlier, so nobody would remember how or why it was; they would rely on the computer records." Sybil paused and remembered who she was talking to. "Nobody human, anyway, but they don't have ems on Corsa, right?"

"Let's hope that's still true. Once he gets there, and they know he's established safely, someone from the local cell can get in contact with him. They can nudge people as needed, remind them of the importance of being on their best behavior around trade diplomats, even if the pirates don't remember inviting him and just want him gone as soon as possible. We'll need Esther to send a message to them, so they can be prepared. They should receive it shortly before he arrives."

"Wait, I decoded the passage in the book. Can't we send the message ourselves?"

"Think about what you're saying," said Pollux. "You decoded it. How confident are that nobody else would be able to? Especially someone as paranoid as a pirate warlord, who probably doesn't get too many incoming communication threads in the first place, so he'll have people analyzing every single one. I assume that code wasn't meant to be unbreakable, just to deter casual readers who might stumble upon the book; we can't risk an interception. Besides, the people we're sending it to might be suspicious about a message in the book code, wondering if it's some enemy that decoded it as you did trying to flush them out."

Sybil wanted to slap herself for not having thought of that

herself. She was irritated at the suggestion that the problem she
had solved wasn't such a hard one, but she realized Pollux was
probably right. It was going to take her some time to get back
into the right frame of mind for conspiracy thinking. "All right.
Good thing we have enough time then. I guess I'll have to go
back to the monastery before we leave then?"

"Yes, I think that will be best, if you don't mind. It's safer
than sending a remote message to Esther, and we have time
before the ship is scheduled to leave. Plus, it will give you a
chance to say goodbye, if that matters."

Sybil tried to think of all the people that might miss her, or
even notice she was gone, but she drew a blank.

"It doesn't really," she said. "What do I have her tell
them?"

"Esther will know what to say. Just let them know a man is
coming, one that can open the door for them."

Sybil backed away from the terminal and stood up.
"Okay," she said out loud. "Let's get this over with." With that,
she left the control room and walked back out of the ship to
the space elevator.

For the ride down, Sybil had managed to convince Pollux
not to get her a first class ticket, so she didn't have a private
compartment; as much as she had appreciated the solitude on
the way up, she was ready for a more plebeian journey back
down. She was placed in a cabin with a young family, the pair
of toddlers keeping their faces pressed up against the glass, still
oohing and ahhing at the views of the planet below even
though they had probably spent the last two couple days seeing
those same views on the way up—she knew putting such small
children in suspension pods was usually frowned upon, so she

assumed they were just there for the elevator ride rather than new arrivals to Alara. She hoped their sense of novelty would last long enough to keep them from getting too cranky on the ride down. The other two passengers in her section both seemed happy to sit quietly by themselves, which was fine by Sybil as well; she hadn't paid attention to where other ships had recently come in from, and she didn't really care.

Even with other passengers nearby, though, she was able to tune all of them out, quiet her senses, and focus on her own thoughts. She spent her time thinking about what she had just gotten herself into. Sure, the plan was probably doomed, but as far as she could tell, she wasn't actually putting herself at risk. At worst, she would find a ship from Sittian back to Alara. More likely, she would just settle into a new life at Sittian, and hopefully enough time would have passed that she could avoid any unfortunate consequences of her past deeds. But what she was really thinking about was this pair of quantum-linked ems. She had never heard of anything like that before. It was hard for her to believe it was even possible, and what Pollux had mentioned about the ways people might take advantage of it, that was just the beginning.

She imagined the kinds of remote hacks she could pull off with a faster than light communication channel, even if one end of the link would need to move slower than light to get into place first. She would easily regain and surpass her previous reputation for financial sabotage and other informational intrusions. And if she could find a way back to the Eleusinian Totem and try to replicate what had happened to Methuselah, she would be unstoppable. Of course, it would be much easier if she could convince Pollux/Castor to work with her, but she knew that was an unlikely possibility, given what she knew about them, how they had stood up to Phoenix and foiled her plan. So she would need to hack them first. Not a hack, really, but social engineering—finding a way to get them to pass coded instructions while they thought they were helping.

The test would be on Corsa, she thought. There she would be expected to be using the linked ems as a communication link. She could try to slip something in, something that might sabotage the mission but not be noticed by the ems or traced back to her directly. Not that she cared one way or the other about Herne's mission, but that would be the way to prove out whether she had a workable technique. Then, if that proved to be successful—oh, so sorry about Herne, we did our best, let's try something over on this planet now—she would be in business. Yes, Esther had been right, she thought. Simply imagining the possibilities ahead of her was exciting her beyond anything she could even remember feeling. It had been so long, but the whole galaxy was opening up to her now, and by the time her elevator reached the planet surface, she knew she was going to make it hers.

Chapter 16

Sybil walked through the town again, but it was different somehow now. Every face she saw, she wondered whether they somehow knew what she knew about the monastery and how long they had been hiding it. Or could they see it in her face, the knowledge that marked her as an insider? And if they could see that, did they see what else she had learned now, and the thoughts and schemes that were going through her own mind?

A group of children ran out of an alley, and she jumped back half a step. But they were just chasing each other in some kind of complicated game involving various dinosaurs, gone before she could fully understand it. A woman wearing a low-brimmed hat looked familiar, but she just nodded as Sybil walked by, and Sybil realized that hat style was in fashion and she had probably seen a dozen or more similar ones on the space elevator. As she passed the bookstore she kept her eyes averted from its windows; she didn't want to know if the store owner was watching her, wondering what direction she might give him regarding the book he had given her.

Back at the monastery, Sybil made her way straight to the elders' room. She didn't need to explain her absence to anyone; nobody that she saw in the halls gave any indication that they had even noticed she was gone for a few days, and it wasn't unusual for people to go walkabout for that long or even much longer. It also wasn't strange for someone to leave abruptly and not return; newcomers might decide the monastic life wasn't really meant for them and fall back into their old habits, and older ones—Sybil now realized—might have left for reasons related to the organization's plots. That would certainly be the case for her leaving, after all, and she expected that everyone would pay as little attention to that as she had to others' departures.

The elders were in session, and she didn't want to interrupt. While she assumed that all the elders were in on the secrets—that was certainly implied by what she had decoded in the book—she didn't want to rely too much on that assumption. Nor did she want to raise a question in anyone's mind about whether she would be suited for this task. They might not be able to stop Pollux from using her now, since he really needed someone with her background immediately, but they could make her future plans more difficult if they had any cause for suspicion. So she stayed back, respectfully out of earshot, pacing the grounds until the meeting broke up and she could approach Esther.

"Can we speak?" she asked. "Privately?"

"Of course," Esther replied, and she ushered Sybil into the room the others had just vacated. "Did you talk to Pollux?"

"I did, and there's a lot I still don't understand. Why are you so interested in Corsa?"

Esther nodded and sighed. "I'm afraid, Sybil, there is much I can't tell you, not until you have been inducted into the elders. But if you go with him and help on this mission, when you return I will personally handle your initiation ceremony."

Sybil wondered how much she should admit to knowing already, and decided that if there were things Esther didn't want to tell her, there was no reason to reveal that some of them were no longer secrets.

"Fine," she said. "I will look forward to that. For now, before I leave, we need you to send a message there. Tell them Herne will be arriving in approximately 84 years—I assume you or they can adjust for the time it will take them to receive the message. And they will have other help. Pollux said you will know what else to say, to convince them to prepare appropriately."

"Yes," Esther agreed, nodding. "I will make sure they get the message and know it is from us. Eighty-four years … maybe I won't be able to welcome you back myself, but you never know."

Sybil realized she had no idea how old Esther—or any of the other elders—really were. She hadn't paid close enough attention to notice if any of them had died in her time there; as far as she could tell they just continued on unchanging. Did they use suspension pods or some other technology when she wasn't looking? Had they perfected a neuro-biological link triggered by meditation that stopped the aging process? Most likely, she thought, it was the obvious, that she just hadn't cared enough to notice.

Anyway," Esther continued, "thank you for your help. Is there anything else?"

"Not from you. But may I use the comm room once more to let Pollux know I am on my way back?"

"Absolutely." Esther went and unlocked the door for Sybil. "Do you need voice, or will text suffice?"

"Text would be fine."

"I'll open the channel for you. Then I'll have to excuse myself, as I have some other responsibilities to attend to. Please close the door when you're done. And good luck on your mission. I hope that you return soon and safe."

"I do too," replied Sybil, and Esther turned and left the room.

That was exactly what Sybil had wanted, but she hadn't dared hope that Esther would actually trust her enough to leave her alone with the communication terminal. She quickly sent off the message to Pollux—one he didn't really need to receive, since he knew how long it would take her to get to the monastery and back up the space elevator. Then, after checking over her shoulder to make sure Esther really wasn't standing there watching her, she entered a quick bit of code to hijack the encryption routines on this terminal. Any messages sent would still be encoded, but it would also attach instructions for the Corsan cell to install an additional agent, one she would be able to tap into when the time came, in the hope that they would do so without any questions. Plus, a separate copy —using a quantum encryption routine that only she could decode—would be sent to Pollux. She didn't think he would question why Esther would send her a private message; given all the secrecy around the monastery's activities, she doubted that he knew everything they were up to, and it wouldn't be surprising that Esther had sent additional instructions for her eyes only.

With that complete, she left the room and carefully closed

the door as Esther had instructed her. The elders' room was unoccupied, but she saw nothing in it that warranted further skullduggery. It was little different than her own cell other than its size; tapestries on the wall, an empty table in the center, and a few scattered chairs that seemed as if they weren't used frequently enough to bother arranging. Electric lights were built into the ceiling, but most of the light at the moment was natural, filtering in through the stained glass windows and skylights. She walked down the stone hallways knowing that, despite Esther's wishes, she would not be returning here. She stopped for one last look in her own room, but as Pollux had said at the beginning, there was nothing there for her.

Knowing it would likely be her last time walking through the town, and not just the town but on Alara at all, Sybil thought that should make her feel free. Instead, she felt even more paranoid than when she had walked to the monastery just hours before. She felt certain that some elder must have noticed what she had done and started following her, waiting for her to take some other action to betray her guilt. The worst part for her was remembering the last time she had felt like this —on Olympia, seeing the man in black everywhere she looked and convincing herself it was all in her imagination. But that had been real, he had in fact been tracking her, so now there was no mantra she could recite to convince herself that it was mere paranoia this time. She wouldn't fool herself a second time.

That was exactly what she was thinking when she entered the base of the space elevator, arranged for her ticket again, and saw a crowd of people who had just come down from the top on their way out. There was nothing about them that would have seemed out of the ordinary to anyone that had seen similar crowds on many a planet before, as Sybil had. Nothing, that is, except that two of them shifted ever so slightly as her eyes glanced their way, hiding behind the people in front of them. It might just have been a case of mild vertigo, adjusting to the planet's gravity, but to Sybil it seemed far too practiced, like someone trying to appear natural but not quite making it.

She was tempted to keep staring at them until they left, but she was afraid to draw too much attention to herself. If she was just being overly paranoid, if they were agents but on some mission other than looking for her, the last thing she wanted to do was make them suspicious of her in any way. So she let her gaze pass over them and started walking to her gate, looking all around as she did, making her own best impression of a provincial Alaran on her first trip to the space elevator, overwhelmed by everything she saw.

There! Out of the corner of her eye, she saw them slip out of the crowd and start following her. She hadn't seen them clearly, but they didn't look like the two that had caught her back on Olympia, and besides, she had killed at least one of them, hadn't she? Sybil had to make a quick decision whether to stay in the public areas, hoping her pursuers would try to avoid making a scene, or find a maintenance hallway and make an escape. She chose the hallway, slipping through a door that a janitor had let close too slowly behind him. Her heart was beating hard, but she tried to stop and breathe and figure out what she was going to do now. Staying on this planet was obviously not an option, assuming they really were after her and it wasn't just a misunderstanding, a theory she wasn't willing to test. Somehow she was going to need to make it onto the elevator and up to the *Hispaniola*, where Pollux would keep her safe. She could rule out the possibility that this was a trap he had arranged, at least; if it was a hoax, it seemed far more elaborate than was necessary, and given that he had tracked her down here, he could have simply sent people to the monastery to capture her. She was confident she could find a back way through these halls to get on the elevator, but what if they followed her? Or circled back and were waiting for her on board already?

Those worries passed when she heard the door crash open and two pairs of running footsteps coming toward her. She took off as quickly as she could, wondering at every door she passed whether it would provide a safe way out, slow her down too much if it turned out to be locked, or trap her in a dead end. At least the corridor wasn't straight—she always had at least one corner between her and her pursuers, so they wouldn't see if she made a turn—but nothing looked promising enough to make her pause, and she knew her own footsteps were echoing as loudly as theirs.

Until suddenly they stopped. It took Sybil a few seconds to realize it, and even after she did, she didn't dare slow down herself, but their last steps had been somewhat louder than the others, and then there weren't anymore. If they knew the elevator terminal better than she did, they might have found an exit that would bring them around in front of her. Perhaps one had stayed behind in case she reversed her own tracks, and the other would be bursting through a door right ahead of her any moment. If that was the case, she thought, she might as well stop running, so she stood quietly and listened for any hint of what might be happening. It was an eerie silence, full of subtle sounds like leaves rustling that might just have been the air vents whistling. Sybil started slowly tiptoeing back around the corner, careful not to hug the wall too closely in case there was an ambush waiting for her.

She passed the first corner without incident, but there was only a short stretch of hall before a second one, so she approached it just as carefully. When she turned again, she saw two bodies lying on the floor, throats slit and blood pooling around them. Looking up, she thought she saw a trace of a shadow on the far wall of the next corner, but it was gone before she could be sure. She started running again, pausing only to confirm that the two corpses were the same two men she had noticed in the crowd. She wondered who they were, and why they were after her—her best guess was that someone had been tracking the *Hispaniola*, hoping it would lead to her if she was still alive, and they had noticed her when she had gone up the elevator the first time—but she was even more curious about who had killed them.

"Hey!" she called down the hallway, hoping to stop the mysterious interloper. "Who are you? What's going on?" She started running again, hoping to catch up but not even hearing footsteps.

She was out of breath when she could see the door that she had used to escape the main plaza in the first place, which stood hanging open and half off its hinges, proof that the two had forced it open rather than having regular access here. Knowing that her benefactor could have easily disappeared into the crowd by now, she turned and walked back to where she had left the bodies, hoping they would at least provide a clue. But when she got to the spot where she was certain they had been, there was no sign of what had happened. No corpses, not even a single drop of blood; if she looked closely, she could see what appeared to be fresh mop marks and trails of cleaning fluid that hadn't quite evaporated completely, but she couldn't be certain they hadn't been there already, and a regular passerby wouldn't have noticed even that much. Shaken, and disappointed that no answers would be forthcoming, she slowly and cautiously walked back to the broken door, entered the milieu of ignorant passengers, and proceeded to her seat in the elevator itself.

* * *

The ride up the space elevator was tense this time, with Sybil always on the watch for another pursuer. But nobody accosted her; neither did anyone appear to explain who it was that helped her below. After a few days, she reached the top again, and as quickly as possible she re-entered the *Hispaniola*.

"Esther confirmed that the message has been sent," Pollux said as she crossed the threshold of the airlock. "She also left a private message for you. We're all loaded, crew is activated, and we are scheduled to depart as soon as you're ready."

"Let's go then, get this over with," Sybil replied. She was reluctant to tell Pollux what had happened, unsure as she was about his possible involvement in it, but she figured she had to trust him at this point. "Two people were chasing me at the bottom of the elevator. Do you know anything about that?"

"Certainly not," Pollux answered. "I suppose it could be just coincidence, but I'm sorry if I inadvertently led them to you. They won't be able to stop us from leaving, though."

"No, they certainly won't," Sybil said with a smirk. "They're both very dead now."

"You killed them?"

"No, someone else did. I don't know who. But I suspect the monastery, or someone associated with it, was looking out for me."

"Yes, that wouldn't surprise me. Especially after you agreed to this trip, Esther would have made sure you arrived safely. And I'm glad you did. Now, before we leave, do you want to go into suspension right away or stay out here for the first part of the journey?"

She stopped to think about this for a while. On the one hand, it had been decades since she had done any space travel, and it really could be beautiful. She still remembered some of what she had seen when she entered the Alara system, but barely. On the other hand, if this was her new life transition, she wanted a clean break as soon as possible.

"I've seen enough. I'll just go into the suspension pod. Wake me when you're ready for me to act."

"Done," said Pollux. "You're the only passenger on this leg of our journey—for obvious reasons, I turned down any others —and Ani will make sure your pod is in perfect condition. Enjoy your rest."

Sybil found the chamber with the suspension pods, climbed in, and closed the door on herself, relieved that she had actually made it without incident and could now forget the feelings of fear that had begun to plague her. Feeling the chamber kick in, for the first time in a long time for her, reminded her of who she used to be, and it felt right, felt like who she really was, and then she was out.

Gemini

Chapter 17

Herne came to and found himself in yet another cell. Unlike the two he had been kept in by Solomon, this one had walls made of rough stone, as if they were in a natural cave somewhere under the mountains. In one spot he could even see a trickle of water coming down from the ceiling, though that didn't mean much; it wouldn't be the first prison cell that had leaky pipes. There was a musty smell, but, again, he couldn't rule out the possibility that it was coming from him and his companions after being crammed together for so long in so many different environments. It was warmer than he would have expected in a cave, but they could have been deep enough that they were completely isolated from the outside environment, and he had no idea how much geothermal energy might be in that region.

He could see most of his fellow prisoners from the truck, including the boy whose leg had been shot; his wound had been bandaged, and he seemed to be resting quietly, and Herne was happy to see that he hadn't been left behind to die. He knew the Corsan guards would have done that, so whoever had taken them now at least had some humanity. He recognized a few of the guards as well, though they had been stripped of their weapons and most of their uniforms, leaving them in simple tunics like Herne and the other prisoners had been forced to wear. Here, wherever this was, they were all equals.

He saw no sign of his new captors, though, so he looked around to see if any of the other prisoners were awake and might be able to answer some of his questions. On the far side of the cell, the man who had been next to him in the truck seemed to be moving. Not feeling anything restraining him, Herne stood up slowly and carefully made his way across the room, taking care not to disturb everyone else who was still asleep.

"Hello," Herne whispered. "My name is H ... um, Tauno. I never got your name."

"Tauno, huh? Are you the infiltrator?"

"The what?"

"Tauno—clearly a fake name. You're here to spy on us, report anyone who causes trouble. There's always one."

Herne hadn't considered this, and for a second he wondered whether it would be worse to reveal his real mission or to be thought an informant.

"No, I'm not the one, if there even is one," he answered. "But then, that's what I would say, isn't it?"

That at least got a small smile out of the man. "My name is ... Jan," he said. Herne nodded in acknowledgment, having no desire to offend the man by asking whether the offered name was real or not. Herne hadn't realized how tall Jan was when they had been seated by each other in the truck, nor when they were out in the dark; he had the muscle to match, and a face that would make anyone fear being alone with him

in the dark. Unlike Lei-Tan and some of the others, it was easy
to believe that Jan had actually done something to earn his
imprisonment; Herne suspected this was a man he would need
on his side, whatever might happen here.

"So, Jan, do you know anything about where we are or
how we got here?" he asked.

Jan shook his head. "No, I was knocked out, like everyone
else it seems." He swept his arm around to encompass everyone lying in the cell. "I've only been awake for a few minutes.
At least our lodgings are more spacious than in the palace,
though. And the walls are … more interesting to look at."

"That they are," Herne agreed. "I'm worried about the
guards, though."

"Yes, me too. They won't be happy when they find themselves stuck with us. And stripped, no less."

"And there are many here who won't be happy to see
them, either."

"So are you saying we should protect the guards against
the people, or the people against the guards?" Jan's face when
he said this gave no suggestion about which side he might be
leaning towards.

Herne shrugged. "We may need to do both."

Jan nodded, apparently deeming Herne's answer accept-
able.

Others started to stir, and Herne saw some unfriendly
looks as people noticed the guards in the cell with them. They
were outnumbered by the prisoners here, but they were also
trained. Herne calculated that if it came to a fight, the guards
would probably hold their own against the rest of the group,
some of whom might be legitimate fighters but most of whom

were probably political prisoners or family members of the same. That would mean a lot of pain and injury to go around, whereas cooperation was more likely to be helpful for getting them out of wherever they were. Rather than wait to see what would happen, he decided to try to preempt whatever anyone else might be starting to think about.

Two of the guards were sitting together near the wall, still looking dazed and groggy, and Herne figured that was the best place to start. He walked over to them, turned to face the rest of the crowd, and said, "Look, we're all here together now. We need to figure out where that is and how to get out. Anyone who is willing to help with that, we need to accept. We can deal with the past later," he continued, turning to look at the guards behind him, who both nodded. "But for now, we have a bigger problem."

"It's the yeti," came a small voice.

"What?" Herne asked, looking around to see who had said that.

The boy stood up, leaning hard on his non-injured leg. "The yeti. I heard stories about them. They live in the mountains and eat bad children."

Herne mostly managed to stifle a laugh. Maybe the boy was even younger than he looked. But he tried to sound like he was taking him seriously and asked, "What do you know about these yeti?"

"They're big and hairy and scary. And you need to obey your parents or they'll come and get you. That's all I know."

"They'll come into town and get you? Has anyone ever seen one?"

"My friend Lila said she saw one out her window one

night. She said it looked really mean. She said she knew it wasn't coming for her, but she was hoping it would take her little sister, who had hit her earlier that day."

"Anyone else?" Herne scanned the room, looking for confirmation that this was more than a child's fairy tale, but expecting none.

After a long pause, though, another voice hesitantly offered, "There are tales."

Herne spun again, his eyes landing this time on an old man. "What kind of tales?"

"Centuries ago, there were genetic experiments, merging humans and various animals."

"I know," Herne replied. "I've heard of them on other planets. They started back on Earth, looking for ways to populate planets that were barely habitable but not quite suitable for humans, without having to go through the expense and time of climate modification. None of them were ever viable, though, and once there were a few colonies established, the research was all abandoned."

"Not here," the old man continued. "Here they kept it going, trying to breed not just for survival, but to create a warrior class or creatures that could more easily subjugate slaves."

"Still, they couldn't have succeeded, not where all the civilized planets failed."

"We're civilized enough, thank you, *outsider*."

Herne swallowed. "Yes, sorry, of course. But are you saying they did succeed here?"

"The stories my grandparents passed on, after my grandfather had been away on the ships for a long time, he said that they had merged humans and a kind of bear. The resulting creatures had survived, but they were rebellious, couldn't be ordered as easily as human soldiers. And as the pirate captains proved capable of managing as many slaves as they needed here, and the so-called *civilized* planets left us alone so we had no need for defense, they were killed off. But the stories say that some managed to escape the city, to hide here in the mountains."

"To steal bad children?" Herne couldn't resist a wry smile.

"No," the man answered seriously. "They never come into the city. But rumors do say that people disappear from Mavros and some of the other mountain mines. That's why they keep sending new rounds of prisoners there, why they need to make excuses to arrest us." He paused and seemed to think about what he had just said. "Of course, plenty of people die there for other reasons, too, I'm sure."

"And you think people disappear because of these human-bear hybrids, these yeti? And that's what captured us?"

"Yeti is just a silly name for them that kids use. All I'm saying is there are stories. I don't know their truth."

"Well, I guess we will know soon enough. Hey!" Herne started to yell. "Whoever's out there! Show yourself!"

There was complete silence among the group, everyone holding their breath as if they actually expected a response. But there was no answer, and when the moment passed, some people started talking quietly to their neighbors, others continued to sit alone, and Herne was pleased to see there was no overt hostility between the guards and the others, all equally prisoners now.

"Thanks," whispered one of the guards. Herne recognized him as the one that had complained about the smoking in the truck, though he had never heard his name. "We were just doing our job, you know."

Herne turned to face him. "Don't think that makes me okay with you," he replied. "Just because I want to avoid a riot that could turn out bad for all of us doesn't mean I'm on your side."

The guard's smile fell, but he dropped his head in acknowledgment. He looked even more tired than he had in the truck, and he was probably the oldest of the six soldiers; maybe he really was regretful for what he had done, Herne thought. The guard next to him, though, kept a stern face, looking straight at Herne with his eyebrows creased. "Don't think this makes me okay with you," he taunted. "Just because you stopped a riot doesn't mean I'm on the side of you low-life criminals. Once we're rescued...." He spat at Herne, who quickly looked around to make sure nobody who might take offense on his behalf had noticed.

"That's enough, Terence," the first guard said. "You know we've never been able to find these caves."

Herne turned back to him. "You mean, you've looked for them?"

"Oh yes," the guard replied. "Well, not me personally, but the stories are real. There's never been a massive search, but every generation or so, someone goes missing, the yeti are blamed, and some young captain decides to make a name for themselves by hunting them down. It's never succeeded. The search party usually ends up dead in the mountains, found months later. At best, they return empty-handed and ridiculed."

"Oric won't fail, though," said Terence. "You know he's

been wanting to do this, planning an excursion, and waiting for the opportunity. It wouldn't surprise me if he triggered the avalanche, just to give him an excuse."

The other guard laughed. "Yes, that sounds like something Oric would do, the bastard. And if it had accidentally crushed us, oh well, it's nothing to him. My name is Aarn, by the way," he said to Herne, holding out his hand.

Herne took the offered hand. "Call me Tauno."

"Yes, I know all about you, *Tauno*," Aarn laughed again. "Terence here is right about one thing, though. If Oric does manage to find us, and I don't believe he will, but if he does, we're not going to be able to be friends. But until then, I hope we can be."

Just then, Herne heard a shuffling behind him. He turned and saw a large shadow appearing around the corner. The shadow then made way for a large, eight-foot-tall man-beast covered with thick white hair. Everyone in the cell was watching it, and everyone took a step back, or ran all the way to the wall, or simply cowered in fear where they stood. It came to the door, and another shadow started growing into the room.

"REORR!" the yeti roared.

"RAREH UOR UR!" a response came from the second shadow, which turned into a similar looking creature, this one carrying a very large gun.

"REOUR REOUR!" the first yeti continued, and it took keys out of a pocket on a belt it wore and began to unlock the cell door.

Chapter 18

Herne just watched as the creature by the door growled and waved them all toward the exit. Nobody was brave enough to take the first step forward, though. They all hung back, afraid to believe that there could possibly be any safety in approaching such a beast.

"REOUR!" it cried again, but that just caused the prisoners to take another step further from the door. The erstwhile guards were acting no more courageous than anyone else, and Herne was on the verge of deciding that he would be the first to move forward, when he saw the boy had beaten him to it, shuffling from the far corner of the cell. Aarn's mouth gaped open, and Herne saw a shameful look cross his face as he ran ahead, not willing to let a mere boy, an injured one no less, show more courage than he had. Herne was in no hurry to prove himself, but he followed slowly behind Aarn, his curiosity beginning to overpower his fear. After all, if the yeti had wanted them dead, they could have shot everyone already, or merely left them all to freeze on the mountain road, so he figured it couldn't really be worse to follow them now. One by one, everyone made a similar calculation, or decided that they didn't have much choice; either way, they all exited the cell.

If the stories Herne had heard were correct and the yeti really were bear-human hybrids, it was clear to him that the bear had gotten the better part of the deal. It wasn't just their physical size, though the two that had come to the cell towered over every man and woman there. Nor was it only their heavy coat of white fur, thick enough for them to not wear any clothing, which caused Herne to turn away in embarrassment when he realized he was standing next to a male and caught himself staring in a rather impolite manner. Their scent was heavy and musky and clearly non-human. Only their head showed any real resemblance to their primate ancestry, and even that would be hard to recognize from a distance under all the facial hair. But their eyes betrayed their intelligence, staring deeply at each prisoner that walked past them.

They followed a third yeti through a passageway until they reached a large dining hall. This room was somewhat bigger than the holding area they had woken in, but it was otherwise similar, with rough-hewn walls and the occasional rivulet tracing a path down them, and not a hint of natural light. In other words, it had all the signs of being deep inside a cavern, like where the yeti were said to live in the old tales. Herne stopped in amazement when he saw the spread laid out in front of him. It was finer than anything he had seen since his arrival on Corsa, and for a man who had been on prisoner's rations for the last two days, it was nearly unimaginable. He could see that the people behind him were having similar reactions; mouths hung open, eyes watered, and faces looked like they were trying to decide between rushing to the table and running away from an obvious trap. Herne wondered how the yeti had managed such delicacies, if they truly were underground. They had some sort of goat, it appeared, and those likely lived in the mountains, or at least nearby. But did they keep poultry here in the caves? The fruit probably came from trees growing wild at the base of the mountains, where the desert gave way to the ocean, but Herne wasn't sure enough about their current location to be able to estimate how far away those might be. And bread implied some kind of grain, which would have to be cultivated in order to allow such amounts; he had no idea how that was being achieved.

For the moment, though, he was willing to put aside all his questions; he sat down eagerly yet politely and began to eat. A few of the others hung back still, but most appeared to have followed Herne's ultimate logic, or something like it, that even if this was a trap of some kind, they couldn't ask for a better last meal. And with a nudge and a growl from the yeti, the laggards finally joined in at the table. The meal was unusually quiet, though, thought Herne; with a spread like that, he expected laughter and jovial conversation, a celebration of the bounty that fate had provided. Instead, there was silence, each man or woman keeping to themselves. The yeti merely loomed over them, either having eaten first or planning to later. Perhaps they couldn't even eat the food here, Herne thought, but that would have made it even more peculiar that they had prepared it for their captives.

The appearance of the feast had stunned everyone, but the flavors were even more incredible to Herne. The meat was incredibly tender, with a rich, earthy tasting mushroom sauce. A cave was the perfect environment for that ingredient, and Herne hoped he would have an opportunity to enjoy more varieties. The fruit was drizzled with the sweetest honey he had tasted, and he gave up trying to figure out where the bees were kept. If the yeti had fruit orchards, then they would need something to pollinate them, so why not collect honey also. There was a thick, buttery tea to wash everything down, a flavor he recalled from his childhood, though he hadn't liked it as much then. Now he couldn't imagine a more delicious beverage, unless the yeti made mead from their honey.

After everyone had their fill, a few more roars and growls from the yeti led them back to their cell. There the talking began. Herne tried to stand back and listen, nodding respectfully when people came up to him and shared how grateful they were for the generosity of their new hosts, and nodding just as respectfully at those who grumbled that they were, after all, still prisoners, and how wrong their captors were if they thought they could be pacified with one nice meal. Nobody actually asked him for his opinion, and he didn't feel the need to volunteer it.

The conversations grew louder as the day passed—at least, Herne assumed it was a day, though there was no real indication of sunrise or sunset within the cave, and he couldn't be sure that when they had first woken it had been morning. Within hours, they had split into two factions, most of them smiling, with hopeful looks on their faces, discussing how their imprisonment was certain to end soon, and how happy they would be to return to their loved ones and tell them what had happened. About a third of the group, though, was different; they were scowling and had descended into whispers that Herne couldn't overhear. He could imagine what they were talking about, though: there was no going back, as they would simply be arrested again and probably blamed for what had happened, and the yeti would probably not free them anyway, since the sure knowledge of their existence would be a tremendous threat to them, and besides, how dare they keep them in a shared cell like this and treat them like mere prisoners. Herne stayed close to the first group, learning more about the local traditions from Lei-Tan and Masud, the man that had first confirmed the boy's stories about the yeti.

"*His* grandfather Paulo had been one of the first colonists here on Corsa," Masud was saying, telling yet another tale from his grandparents. "And the story Paulo told him, which he then passed on to me, was how great it was to find a frontier again. Earth had gotten too crowded and anyone who wanted to live a little wilder was stifled into conformity. The first settlements seemed to offer a chance, but the realities of terraforming meant they could only occupy a small area on the planets, at least at first, and the same Earth elites quickly dominated those societies. It was such a relief for them to find this hunk of rock that nobody wanted, to turn it into their own free society."

"Free!" Lei-Tan spat. "Nobody here is free except for Solomon's cronies. And your grandfather was a pirate captain, so you're tainted, too."

Masud grew red in the face. "Not a captain. He was conscripted, too young to know any better, he would tell me. But he revered Paulo and the other originals, as he called them, fleeing civilization—not that we're not civilized here, Tauno."

Herne just nodded, knowing that anything he might say here would just dig a deeper hole for himself.

"Fleeing *so-called* civilization to create a better form of civilization. Even if it hasn't turned out that way over the years."

At that point, Aarn approached and tapped Herne on the

shoulder, beckoning him to break away from the crowd and speak in private.

"Sorry to interrupt," Aarn whispered. "I'm afraid there might be some disturbance at our next meal."

"What do you mean, disturbance?"

"I don't know exactly," Aarn replied. "Terence was sounding me out for something, but I don't think he fully trusts me, and I've just got no energy for feigning interest and playing the spy, let alone for whatever he has in mind."

"I totally understand," Herne said, nodding. "Let's be on the watch, then. But why are you telling me?"

"You seem like a solid fellow, someone who will help keep the peace, and strong enough to force a peace if needed. There was another with you earlier, right, making sure nobody started any trouble?"

"Yes." Herne paused to remember the man's name. "Jan. I'll give him a heads-up, too."

"Thanks. It may be nothing, but we should be ready in case."

"Agreed."

At some point in time—Herne assumed it was evening—the yeti returned and led them back to the dining hall, where a similar spread awaited them. This time the main course was some kind of fish—it was big enough to have come from the ocean, but it was hard to believe the yeti would go that far rather than catch them in the streams that flowed out of the mountains. The fish was accompanied by another incredible array of delicacies: root vegetables glazed with a spice blend Herne couldn't place, more tender mushrooms, and berries and goat-milk cream. Herne noted that the seating at the table now mirrored the segregation that had occurred during the day in the cell, with the unhappy folks clustered at one end of the table. And while people at Herne's end were beginning to relax and chat freely as one would expect at a shared meal like this, the other end remained as silent as they all had originally.

Herne found himself sitting by Jan, a quiet young woman named Aster, and a man who still refused to share his own name. "Call me 'Hey You,'" he had told Herne, and he refused to be pressured beyond that. Other than that, though, he was happy to dominate the conversation.

"Oh yeah, there are lots of fish out there in the ocean," he said. "I used to go out on the boats regularly, caught much bigger ones than these river trout." He swung his hand to include everything that was on the table.

Herne was only half listening, though. He had heard plenty of fish stories in his life, and he knew what his role was, so he nodded and expressed awe at the appropriate times. Meanwhile, his attention was on the rest of the table, watching for any indication that the trouble Aarn had warned about might be starting.

"This one fish was three times my size, nearly knocked my boat over!" Herne gave him the obligatory eye raise. "And I don't know how you Olympians do it, but we catch our fish the old fashioned way, none of those 'humane' stun guns that any monkey could use. I had to spear the beast and lift it out of the water myself."

Herne wasn't sure if he would need to respond on behalf of Olympians, but there was hardly a gap for him to say a word before the man continued with his bragging.

When dinner was over and the yeti signaled it was time to

stand up and leave, Terence nodded and made a motion with his hands, a prearranged signal of some sort. The people around him—three other guards, if Herne recognized them correctly, and two that had originally been prisoners—started a sequence of choreographed movements. Three of them ran straight at the yeti that was standing guard with a gun while two others circled toward the one by the door; all of them were carrying knives from the table. Meanwhile, Terence stood and exhorted the rest of the group to join in the rebellion. "Don't be collaborators!" he cried. "Rise up! We can control our own destiny!"

Herne was having none of that, though. He glared at Terence, then glanced over at Aarn and made a hand motion of his own. Aarn nodded in understanding, and the two of them rushed the man who had started the riot. He appeared shocked, as if he had expected that everyone else would naturally see things his way or at least sit cowardly neutral, and by the time he had recovered, Aarn and Herne were already there, pinning his arms behind him and holding a knife of their own against his throat.

"Stop the uprising! Defend our hosts!" Herne made his own exhortations now that Terence was silent; though they seemed poor in comparison, he hoped they would be enough to stop people from unthinkingly following Terence as the only option.

More people moved away from the table now. From Herne's side, Aster ducked under the table, but Jan led the nameless fisherman and two others towards the door to defend the yeti there. They grabbed the two attackers as they slashed at the creature, trying to deflect its powerful arms and sharp claws while avoiding being pulled away by Jan and his cohort. At the same time, the rioters managed to strip the gun away from the other yeti, and Herne recognized Zara, the guard that had started smoking in the truck, holding it now, sweeping it back and forth between the yeti her co-conspirators were holding down and the action going on in the rest of the room.

"Let Terence go!" she shouted at Herne and Aarn while aiming the gun in their direction.

"No! Drop the gun!" Aarn replied, keeping his knife pressed tight at the man's throat, a thin red line beginning to appear on the surface of his skin. He and Herne were both careful to keep Terence between them and the gunner, hoping she wouldn't be willing to shoot through him in order to kill the two of them.

Jan's group had subdued their two opponents, and he called for others to go after the gun, which Zara was now pointing at the yeti by the door, keeping it from approaching her. But everyone who hadn't already chosen sides was either hiding quietly or screaming in terror, either way unwilling to join in the melee. And their screams could barely be heard over the roars of the yeti; Herne had no idea whether they were cries of anger, calls for assistance, or some combination of those and more.

It didn't take long for that assistance to come, though, in the form of three more yeti carrying rifles and wearing protective armor. It quickly became clear the situation had changed, and not to the benefit of those who had wanted to escape. Zara's mouth dropped open, and she dropped the gun and put her hands up; her accomplices immediately followed suit. The yeti who had been standing by the door went over to his two attackers, pinned to the floor by Jan and his helpers. They jumped out of the way and quickly retreated as the yeti picked the two up, one under each arm, and carried them off. A series of growls and rough shoves from the newly arrived armed yeti got the three humans who had attacked the gun to follow. That left Herne and Aarn, still holding the ringleader tight.

"RARUOUR ARR!" cried the yeti who had originally held the gun.

"What do you want us to do with him?" asked Herne.

"REOR RARUOUR ARR!" replied the yeti. Herne didn't know what they were expected to do. He was afraid to simply let go, as the guard he was holding might take out his fury on him before facing his own fate.

"RARUOUR ARR!" repeated the yeti, raising a hand to his own throat and moving one finger across it. Aarn got the message, and he inserted his knife into the leader's neck, which was harder with a table knife than it would have been with a proper bayonet, but he was nevertheless able to slash the artery. Herne and Aarn both jumped back to get away from the spouting blood, and the man collapsed to the floor.

The people cowering beneath the table started to emerge, now that the fighting was over. Herne tried to read the reactions on the yeti faces. He hoped they wouldn't blame all the humans for what had happened, that they would recognize the factions and be pleased with those that had resisted the rebellion.

The yeti who had been present through the battle explained the situation to the new arrivals, but all Herne heard was a series of roars, which was useless in helping him understand where he stood. Then one of the yeti pointed at him and indicated that he should follow, and when he found himself led to a private room with what appeared to be a very comfortable, if exceedingly large by human standards, bed, he had his answer. He hoped that Aarn and the others were being treated as well and that the other troublemakers were being shown at least a little mercy, which was more than they deserved. He knew there would be plenty of time to find out later, after things had settled down. For now, just being able to stretch out and enjoy some quiet solitude seemed like a such a luxury to him, and he was going to indulge while he could.

Chapter 19

Days passed, then weeks. Herne enjoyed his room, spartan as it was compared to his lodgings in Solomon's palace —it was a cave, after all, with rough ceilings and walls undecorated but for the different shades of gray speckles in the rock. It was slightly more spacious than his quarters on the *Umbriago*, though, and certainly more interesting. He had quickly noticed that the bed was not solid as he had imagined at first; instead, it consisted of a stack of furs—not yeti fur, he assumed, but some other large animal that the yeti either raised or hunted— and he could insert himself somewhere in the middle. The only other furnishing in the room was a small wooden desk that he really had no use for, with nobody to write to and nothing to write on or with. The fact that there were rooms for them, and human-size furnishings, was evidence that they weren't the first visitors in the caves, though Herne hadn't dared to ask what had happened to earlier ones, or how long it had been since the yeti had seen humans.

Nearly everyone had since been moved into their own rooms, either immediately with Herne, or eventually when they had proven their worth, or loyalty, or whatever it was exactly that the yeti were looking to reward. Only the five that had taken part in the initial uprising remained stuck in the common cell, but even they had been given beds and some curtains for a bit of privacy. If anything sinister was going on, it would be there, but while Herne still occasionally overheard grumbling at meal times about the general unfairness of it all, there were no specific complaints, and at least it hadn't spilled over into violence again.

* * *

"Is that bed warm enough with just you in it?" Aster asked, standing in the doorway to his room.

This wasn't the first time she had come to seduce him. He knew he wasn't the only one she came to, either. Secrets like that couldn't be kept in their current environment. And everyone had their own way of handling the stress of confinement.

"It's just fine, thank you," Herne answered.

"You and Lei-Tan, right? Or are you saving yourself for some yeti dominatrix?"

Herne looked startled. That was not a line he had expected to hear from her. It reminded him of Gwen, in her wilder moments.

"Oh, come on," Aster continued, letting herself in and sitting down at the desk. "You don't realize that's why we're here? How many yeti do you think there are anyway?"

Herne had to admit he didn't have a good idea; he couldn't tell one from another, so he had no good way to keep track of their numbers. The small ones were obviously children, but he rarely saw them; Herne expected they were mostly kept away from the humans for their own safety. But for the adults, he couldn't even distinguish male and female without looking too closely to be considered polite. Still, he didn't think there were more than a few dozen, maybe a hundred. Barely enough to maintain any kind of genetic diversity.

"I really don't think that's why we're here." He wasn't going to admit to Aster that for a few days, at least, he had considered it as a possibility. "They would have done something by now. As a punishment if nothing else."

"Maybe their women are only fertile in the spring."

"And their men couldn't mate with you just as easily?"

That at least brought a small blush to Aster's face. "So, no then?" she asked after she recovered.

"No, I've got some thinking to do."

In fact, he had been thinking about Castor when she had walked in, wondering whether the em had followed his instructions and gotten out of the system. That had led to wondering how he would ever get off this planet himself if his ship had either left or been attacked. But getting off the planet first required getting out of the cave and away from the yeti, and he still had no idea what the yeti intended to do with them, or if they even had a long-term plan. It didn't feel like they were under house arrest, but even if the yeti were willing to let them leave, he knew it would be ill-advised, given the treacherous hike through the frigid mountain passes that would be required to reach any other kind of shelter.

At least he got to explore the cave system, which was much more intricate than he had imagined. He suspected it wasn't all natural, either; there must have been something for them to hide in at first, simply to survive, but he was pretty sure they had expanded the tunnels over the centuries. He had yet to find a clear seam, though, between the natural and the yeti-made, and until he did, he couldn't be certain he was right about that. He never saw an actual power plant, either, but he understood they were using some combination of geothermal and fusion-generated electricity. That enabled heating, lighting, and air recirculation, letting them grow a variety of plants and animals out of sight of any surveillance while not infringing on their living space.

Over the course of his wanderings, he had identified many of the foods they had eaten, too, putting an end to most of that mystery. Goats may have lived wild in the mountains, but the yeti didn't rely on that. They had their own pens of domesticated animals in the caves, along with multiple species of fowl. A vast open space had been created for fields of grain, to make bread and feed the animals. In some places, it was barely high enough for the yeti farmers to stand up in, and in others the ceiling was so high as to be invisible without directing a light at it, but either way, it was enough for the crops to grow. He even found the apiary, at the end of a cave that had cracks large enough for the bees to fly out and pollinate whatever was outside. He assumed the yeti gathered the actual fruit in clandestine excursions outside the caves, along with fish and anything else they didn't grow inside, but he had also found enough storerooms to know that those foraging trips wouldn't need to be too frequent.

* * *

"Listen to this, Tauno!" the boy said as he came running into Herne's room. Herne was happy to see it wasn't Aster again. In the time since that first evening, the boy had come to visit Herne many times, seeming to prefer him over any of the others for some reason. Nika, as he had introduced himself, actually reminded Herne of himself as a child, if he had been raised in a semi-feudal society like Corsa instead of a more civilized planet. (*Yes, more civilized*, he thought, despite what Masud would say.)

"What is it, Nika?"

"ERARE RA ERARERE ERAREUER" Nika growled, then he panted, catching his breath. "I still can't do it quite right, we don't have the vocal cords for it after all, but that was supposed to be, 'The sun is bright today.'"

"Wow!" Herne responded. "Impressive progress already. When will you be able to say, 'How do we go home?'"

"Hey, I'm in no hurry to get out of here," Nika said. "This is the best I've eaten since I can remember. And with my father killed and my mother already at one of the mines, I have no home to go to anyway. Besides, this is fun! You've been to other planets; how many languages do you know?"

Here was some of the same enthusiasm that Herne remembered from his own childhood, though Nika was too young still for that to have translated into the rebellious tendencies that had estranged Herne from his own family. And now, without a family to rebel against, his future would likely turn out to be very different than Herne's, unless the prison experience sent him down a similar path.

"I have to admit, only the one," he answered. "There's enough continuous communication between the planets that the languages don't really diverge. So other than people who study old Earth languages for research—or, as you say, fun—everyone's pretty much speaking the same way. Which is lucky for anyone that travels between them. Heck, even coming back to your own planet after a couple hundred years in a suspension pod would be a challenge otherwise."

Nika shook his head. "Hard to believe. And yet, these guys have been right here for, what, only a thousand years? And they speak completely differently!"

"Yeah, but remember, they've been isolated."

"Not completely," Nika interrupted.

"Sure, they've had other guests over the years, but most of them haven't heard much. Plus, they can't teach each other when there aren't any humans around; with their limited vocal cords, they can't come close to pronouncing most of our sounds."

"And we can barely pronounce theirs. REORUR!"

"That was 'good night,' right?"

"No! More like 'amazing' or 'incredible'. 'Good night' is REOR UR!"

Herne frowned and furrowed his brow. "I can't tell the difference."

"It's a tone thing, and the glottal stops can be tricky. I don't know; maybe you just need more practice listening to it."

"Or maybe I just need younger ears," Herne smiled, getting a husky laugh out of Nika. "Have you had any luck teaching them writing yet?"

"They have writing," Nika said, rolling his eyes.

"I mean some kind of alphabetic system. I can't learn those thousands of pictographs."

"No, I need to understand their sounds a lot better before I could even try. Besides, there's not much to write on up here. The guards had a little paper on them, but their tablets have been smashed already."

"Okay, so speech it is. At least it's better than old-fashioned hand gestures. I'm glad you're making such quick progress."

"Like I said, it's fun!" Nika gave a huge smile, but it quickly changed to a frown. "Plus, there's nothing else to do here."

Herne pondered that and decided it needed a response. While he agreed with Nika that the food was incredible, they couldn't just stay here forever; everyone was growing antsy, and the peace wouldn't last forever. "All right, I guess it's time to come up with a plan."

Chapter 20

W e need a map," Herne said a few days later, then realized that he was alone in his room. He walked down the hall and found Aarn.

"We need a map," he repeated.

"A map of what?" Aarn looked up from his desk, where he was writing something that Herne couldn't see. Herne wasn't sure how he had gotten the paper and pen—perhaps he had some on hand when he was captured, or perhaps Nika had been wrong about the shortage. In any case, Herne still had no one to write to and no interest in keeping a journal of any sort.

"Of their caves, first, and then the trails through the mountains, and the road to the mine."

"Well, that sounds easy enough. Why don't you go ask for one." Aarn turned back to his writing.

Herne paused for a moment. "Aren't you going to ask why I want a map?"

"No, you go do your thing. I'm happy here."

Herne slowly backed out of Aarn's room and continued down the hall.

"Nika, can you help me get a map?" he asked when he had reached the boy's room.

"Sure," said Nika, pausing his exercises. Herne knew that the boy's leg would still bother him a little sometimes, however much he tried to hide it. "I know you're anxious to get out of here. But you understand if I decide to stay, right?"

"Don't you want to hear why I want a map?"

"I guess. I figured you'd start with that, though, if you wanted to tell me."

Herne just shook his head. "Okay. We can't be that far from the mine, right? I swear I could see it around a corner once when we were walking around the avalanche."

"Yeah, but we didn't want to go to the mine, remember? Forced labor? Work till we're dead?" Nika made signs to show just how crazy he thought Herne was. "I know we're isolated here, but we're still better off."

"But they have vehicles there! We can get back to the city!"

"If they don't kill us at the mine first. And even then, that just means they kill us in the city. No thanks."

"They won't kill us at the mine. We just need … the yeti can help us!"

"You think the yeti will expose themselves just to help you steal a car? And don't forget, you're still dead in the city."

Herne took a deep breath. "Okay. My name isn't really Tauno."

Nika started to look more interested. "Obviously."

"And you may have been sentenced because of something your family did—" Herne saw the look on Nika's face and hastened to correct himself. "—or was wrongfully accused of doing. But I'm here on this planet to take out the pirate leadership."

The boy grimaced. "Looks like you're doing a fine job of

it. So you want the yeti to expose themselves so you can steal a car, drive into the city, and get killed for a good cause. Not much of an improvement."

"I have help."

"Not much, or you wouldn't be here."

"Fair point," Herne acknowledged. "How many people do you think are at the mine?" he asked after thinking a bit more.

"I don't know." Nika scratched his chin and rolled his eyes toward the ceiling. "Hundreds? Maybe a thousand? Not counting the guards, of course."

"Of course. The guards will have to all be killed, naturally. Unless Aarn can help convert them."

"So you want the yeti to expose themselves so you can kill all the guards at the mine, steal all the vehicles, and drive a thousand people into the city to be killed."

"I haven't worked it all out yet, okay!"

"Fine," Nika conceded. "But what's in it for them?"

"You don't think they'd want revenge on the people who exiled them?"

Nika stopped and thought for a moment. "Well, I haven't asked them. But that was centuries ago, and they've been happy to stay isolated since then. I doubt you'll have any new argument that could change their minds."

"They must have kept us alive for some reason."

"They're not murderous beasts!" said Nika.

"Of course not, but they didn't have to take us in in the first place. They could have just left us on the trail hiking to Mavros."

Nika gave Herne a skeptical look.

"Look," Herne said, holding out his hands in supplication,

"all I'm asking is for you to help me make my case. Translate for me. If they're not interested in helping, maybe they'll at least give me a chance to leave and try again myself."

"All right. I'll tell them what you want to do."

Together, they left Nika's room and walked into the main conference room where two of the yeti leaders were seated. Herne thought he recognized one of as the yeti who had initially led them to meals and who continued to act as the primary guardian of the human visitors, but he was still not quite sure.

"REOR UR REOR UR!" said Nika. Herne understood that, even though it sounded the same to him as good night or amazing, this was a respectful daytime greeting.

Or at least it was supposed to be. The yeti appeared to laugh for a moment, but then they stood up and responded in kind: "REOR UR!"

Nika stumbled through what Herne hoped was a reasonable translation of his plan and not insults about the yeti's mothers or non-sequiturs about food and weather. When he finished, the yeti stood silently, either considering the plan or wondering how to kill Herne most painfully as a punishment for suggesting it. Herne balled up his left fist and put it against his forehead in what he had gathered was a yeti-style salute.

"Please tell them I would be most honored to have their assistance," he said to Nika, who gave a final sequence of growls.

Herne waited, eyes flitting from one of the yeti to another, until finally, one of them responded with a similar salute and a roar that caused Nika to widen his eyes and nearly jump in excitement.

"He said yes!" he shouted. Then he turned back to the yeti. "ERARARU EROARR?"

"ARRA ERARARU ARR!"

"Yes, not only do you get your map, but they will send their army with you. It's not really much of an army, mind you, but that's the closest word."

"They'll come attack the mine, free the prisoners?"

"And go with you into town, if you need their help there."

"Why?"

"I guess you were right. They know that one of these times, a search foray is going to find them, and they feel their luck is running out. They've been waiting for help, though, because they know if they just show up in the city, it won't go well for them. You're giving them an opportunity to protect their future. Not all of them are thrilled with the idea, but that's the consensus, anyway."

Herne was overwhelmed with astonishment, but he remembered his manners and gave another salute, bowing at the same time. "Tell them, thank you," he asked Nika.

"ROROR!" Nika roared.

The yeti returned to their seats, and Herne didn't need a translator to know that it was time for him to leave.

"So, Nika, when do we put together our plan?" he asked once they were at a respectful distance and wouldn't interrupt the yeti discussion further.

"I'll bring them some paper after dinner tonight. Aarn has some, right? We'll draw out the map and put together the plan. They can be ready in three days if need be."

Three days, Herne thought. He had been hoping for sooner, but that was when he thought he'd be leaving on his own. Now he had to come up with more of a plan first, one that wouldn't just get a whole lot of people killed. But three days would be plenty of time for that planning, given that he had nothing else to do, and he would happily accept the slight delay in exchange for what was now a much greater chance of success.

There were still a couple hours before dinner, but Herne found himself too nervous to go back to his room and rest. Instead, he wandered through the caves, not even paying attention to exactly where he was going, just keeping himself moving and trying to calm himself enough to think. He wanted to keep the news to himself until he actually had a plan put together, but by the time he arrived in the dining room, he knew he had been unsuccessful at that.

Aarn started it midway through the meal: "I hear we're leaving. So I guess you got your map?"

"Yeah, Tauno, are you ditching us?" asked Zara acidly, still bitter because she was sleeping in the main cell, though after the first week, she had stopped overtly condemning Aarn and Herne for the death of Terence. "What's the plan?"

"What's the plan?" echoed around the table.

Herne knew he wasn't going to be able to feign ignorance, not when rumors flew so quickly in their confined space, so he told everyone what he could.

"There's no plan yet. I'm meeting with the yeti leaders tonight to figure that out. But no one is going to be left behind. If you want to leave with me, you are welcome to be part of it." That wasn't entirely true, Herne knew. The original prisoners could, but for the remaining guards, he was going to have to rely on Aarn to judge where their loyalties would lie and whether they could be trusted. Anyone who might betray them would stay here with the yeti or be killed before they left, but Herne wasn't going to say that out loud.

"How will we not get killed back in the city? Where are we going to go? When do we leave? How do you know it's not a trap?" The questions came faster than Herne could answer.

"Look, I'll know more tonight. We'll probably go in three days, but other than that, I'll share the details tomorrow."

That didn't stop the questions, but Herne did his best to ignore them and focus on what he was eating. The meals hadn't been scaled down since their arrival, and even though they were less of a surprise now, they were still just as impressive. In fact, they rivaled some of the feasts at the lodge in Jurassia, after he would return from leading dinosaur hunting trips and treat his clients to a meal they would always remember. Once he left the cave, he didn't expect to be fed anything comparable until he was able to leave Corsa and arrive on some other planet, so he wanted to enjoy it as much as he could.

After dinner, Herne and Nika followed two of the yeti back into the conference room to discuss the plan. Herne had convinced Aarn to follow along as well; even if he was happy here, his understanding of his colleagues' training would be invaluable for preparing the assault, and they needed him to help them determine which of the other ex-guards could be relied on and which were still too dangerous.

"Here's what I have in mind," Herne began, and Nika translated his words into growls for the yeti, though Herne thought that at least one of the yeti was able to understand some of what he was saying directly. It would be helpful if that were the case, he thought, since they wouldn't be completely reliant on Nika's well-intentioned but limited attempts to speak yeti, and they might avoid a critical misunderstanding. But the yeti seemed happy to let everyone else think they were reliant on Nika; Herne knew he would do the same in their position, holding on to any informational advantage he could, and he kept his suspicions to himself.

Hours passed, and it was clear the slow communication was wearing on everyone. Aarn and Nika were sniping at each other, and even the yeti's hairy faces were showing signs of fatigue. But finally, they arrived at a plan that everyone agreed had the best chance of working, with two days for preparation, then departing just before dawn on the third day.

"What do you really think?" Herne asked Aarn privately once they had returned to their own rooms.

"It's desperate," he replied. "Look, you know I'm tired, and I get cranky when I'm tired, so maybe I'll think differently in the morning. But I don't think you have much of a chance. The guards at the mine are well trained. Well, so were we, and the yeti still captured us, but these guys also have fortifications and positional awareness; they're not exposed like we were on the mountain pass. So there will be no quietly picking them off one by one. Either the plan goes perfectly and you shut them all down at once, or you're all dead. There's no room for error."

"And do you think any of your colleagues will join us?"

"I really don't know. I'll start talking to them privately tomorrow, but I think it will be a hard sell. The young ones have too much of a sense of honor—or stubbornness, or both —and the older ones like me will just be too tired."

"I'd still like you to come."

"I know, but I can't. If you succeed, I'll come to your victory celebration. If you fail, I'll stay out here, retired and hidden." He yawned and then put his hand on Herne's shoulder. "Now, good night."

The next morning, as he expected, Herne was peppered with questions again. He explained their goal—they were going to leave, free the workers in the mine, take their vehicles, and drive into the city. He brushed aside questions of tactical details, especially what would happen after the mine—he couldn't betray the existence of Rila's organization—by explaining they were still being fleshed out and that everyone would learn their role. But then came the question he had most feared but knew he would have to answer.

"What about them?" asked Lei-Tan, pointing at two of the guards who had joined in the mutiny on the first day but been quiet since. They hadn't been killed like the leader, Terence, had, but, as with Zara, they were stuck in the common cell and were being watched carefully by both the yeti and the rest of the prisoners. "You know they'll shoot us in the back as soon as we're close to their buddies at the mine."

A rising chorus proved to Herne that this was a major concern, as he knew it would be. All the guards seemed to be making themselves as small as possible, protecting themselves from the mob fury.

"All right," Herne spoke over the noise of the crowd. When it quieted down enough, he continued. "All of us have a past." He raised his voice to speak over the objection he could see someone raising their hand to make. "Even those of us who were imprisoned for nothing have things in our past that we might not be so proud of." The would-be objector lowered his hand and gave a small nod. "So let's give everyone a chance to decide their own future, and to prove that they will be with us and not against us."

"I'll never trust them," Lei-Tan said, and there were a few mumbles of agreement, but nobody was willing to continue the argument publicly.

* * *

After two days of preparation and question answering, their last night in the yeti caves finally came. Herne cornered Aarn privately.

"Have you changed your mind?" he asked.

"No, I'm still staying here. I think there would be an uproar if I came, anyway; too many people would be happy to seek revenge once they're armed, and they won't think of me any differently from the other guards."

"And what about the other guards?"

"None that I think you can trust."

"So?"

Aarn paused before answering. "I'll take care of it. Once the rest of you are gone."

"Thank you." Herne didn't press for exactly what he meant by that; he was pretty sure he didn't want to know the details. "Should we stop back here after the mine, in case you've changed your mind then?"

"No need. But like I said, I'll come to your victory party."

Herne smiled. "Fair enough. Good night."

"And good luck tomorrow," Aarn answered.

Chapter 21

Sybil wondered just how long she should wait.

Everything had gone according to plan at the start. The agent was installed, and the networking protocol it needed was similar enough to what she had started with that it was able to adapt. She had counted on Corsan technology being outdated, but it still could have evolved to be incompatible; luckily for her, that wasn't the case. She waited until Herne had reached the fringe of the system, still a year or so away from orbiting the planet but close enough that a communication link between his ship and the planet would have latency measured in hours, frustratingly slow but usable. Pollux then brought her out of suspension for the first time, and she had been able to use the remote agent to hack into the Corsan leadership's scheduling system and insert backdated entries for an Olympian trade representative to be arriving. The reports that Pollux received from his counterpart Castor a year later, which he passed on to her after waking her again, indicated that the plan had worked: Herne had landed successfully on the planet without being killed immediately.

Then Herne had made contact with the local members of the mysterious organization that she still didn't quite under-

stand—the ninjas, if that's what they were. He had worked
with Castor, and unknowingly with her, to coordinate a plan
that would allow that organization to infiltrate the palace. But
they had suddenly lost contact with him. Then, Castor had
received a broadcast communication from the Corsan leadership that "the spy" had been detained, and they were prepared
to enter hostage negotiations.

She knew something had gone wrong, and after getting
access to the stored security footage, she saw how he had been
captured. But there was still something strange that happened,
that she couldn't explain. Other than the initial contact, there
had been silence from Corsa, no continued requests for ransom, no escalating threats, nothing. It was as if Herne had
dropped off the face of the planet. All she wanted was to keep
Castor and his ship from being blown up before she had figured out how to take advantage of this instantaneous linkage
to a remote planet for her own benefit. At some point, though,
she was going to have to recommend that Castor get out of
there, or he would decide that for himself. Then she would go
back into suspension, never knowing when another opportunity might arise, or if the best she could do would be to sell her
knowledge of the twinned ems to others who might want to
exploit it.

Of course, Pollux knew nothing about her motives, so any
discussion they had about strategy had to be built around the
fiction that she was just trying to help.

"How long has it been?" she asked from her cabin on the
mail ship. She still preferred to avoid the control room—too
many bad memories there—so, since Pollux could contact her
anywhere, she stayed where she was comfortable, and right

now she was stretched out on her bed, kicking her feet in the air and staring at the ceiling.

"Still five weeks since the last contact," Pollux answered. "No new executions planned, at least not public ones. And I'm quite sure that this one would be public."

"Where is Castor now? He left orbit, right?"

"Yes, he moved immediately after being notified that Herne was captured. He's in a higher solar orbit now, shadowing a small asteroid. He's starting to lag behind the planet, but still in close enough range for continuous communication to the ground. No sign of threat to him yet; either they haven't tracked him—unlikely—or they're still unsure what to do about him, maybe watching to see if a larger Olympic fleet is really on its way."

"How much longer do you think that bluff is going to work?"

"I couldn't say, but I wouldn't expect much."

Sybil thought for a while and then, having made a decision, she got up out of bed and walked over to the terminal. "Okay, it's time to reach out to whoever's on the planet there."

"Can you do that?" Pollux asked.

"Yes," Sybil mumbled. "When Esther sent the original coded message from the monastery, I made sure I got a copy of the original and the coded versions, and I figured out the encryption scheme. I was worried it would be some kind of quantum one-time-pad, and it's possible they might get suspicious about an old key, but I'm pretty sure I can get them a message that they'll accept. The question is, is Castor ready for what I have in mind?"

"What is that exactly?" the em answered. Since the two

ems were entangled, Sybil could never be sure if it was Pollux answering for himself or forwarding an answer from Castor, or if there was even a distinction between the two.

"You said he's starting to lag behind Corsa, right? I think we need to get him down there while we can, so we keep local access. If they have a secure way to receive him, he should be able to transfer safely, but it will definitely be a risk."

"Let's do it. If Herne is still alive down there, we need to do whatever we can to rescue him."

That bastard deserves whatever he gets, Sybil thought to herself, but now Pollux was right. Helping him, assuming he was still alive, would keep Castor in place and give her a reason to keep using her link until she had figured out all the details of how it could work to her advantage.

"All right. I'm typing up the coded message. Please have Castor forward it on. They don't need to know exactly where I am or how we're doing this, just that we want them to receive an em."

Once the message was sent, all Sybil could do was wait again. There was no way she could know if it was received, a coded broadcast that anyone in the Corsan system would be able to pick up but only the intended recipient could under-stand. At least, that's what she hoped, assuming that she had done the encryption correctly, that Esther hadn't sent a mes-sage she was unaware of, telling them to ignore any further messages with that code, and that there was even anyone still alive on the planet for her to work with.

But she had to assume all that. The only alternative was to give up, and she wasn't going to do that until Castor and Pollux did, and she knew they wouldn't until either they had some concrete evidence that Herne was dead or a Corsan pirate fleet started to chase Castor out of the system. What she couldn't do, though, was stay cooped up in her room waiting for a response. She went out and started jogging the halls, lap after lap past the shuttle bays that still made her shudder each time she saw them, but at least there was some change of scenery as she went, which was better than the treadmill. This ship simply wasn't designed for a human crew to be active in for an extended period of time, and passengers were normally in suspension for their whole journey, so the experience was spartan at best.

She had just started to work up a sweat when Pollux spoke through a terminal she was passing by. "We have a response," was all he said; he had told her not many of the crew knew about the connection, so she didn't expect any details until she was back in her private quarters, where he had restricted access to the audio interface, keeping their conversations private from the crew. As soon as she got there, Pollux immediately filled her in with the details.

"They gave us full directions for a secure transfer. As soon as we have a sufficiently long guaranteed alignment—well, guaranteed only so long as the Corsans don't decide to hunt down the *Umbriago* at the most inconvenient time possible, now that we've decided to try this—anyway, in about nine hours, we'll have that alignment and start the quantum transfer."

"How long will the transfer take?" Sybil had never seen an em transfer take place through a space link. Moving them from wearables to home systems or even to transportation took a fraction of a second with a good quantum coupler, but she had no idea what it would be like trying it from orbit, let alone however far the ship was from Corsa now. She was beginning to worry that it might be excessively risky, but it was still the best plan available to them as far as she could tell. If the transfer failed, then this project would be over for her, and she would continue on to Sittian ready to start a new life, for better or for worse. Probably for worse, as she remembered the attempted attack on her as she was about to leave Alara; whoever had been behind that would be able to track where she was headed now, and would probably have someone waiting for her when she arrived. But she had enough problems to worry about now, so that one would have to wait.

"At least seventy minutes, if they can maintain maximum transfer rate. Possibly up to a few hours if there is any interference."

"How will that feel for you?" Sybil was honestly curious, forgetting for a second what effect it might have on her own schemes. "Not having contact with half your mind for so long?"

"I … guess I'll find out. I haven't really thought about it."

So it was going to be more waiting, but at least she wouldn't be risking losing her own mind. And once Castor was back online, she had a feeling there would be little time to rest.

Chapter 22

The march was easier in the daylight, compared to Herne's first time through these mountains, when they had left the disabled truck behind them and been force-marched through the darkness. There was none of the fear that had gripped them then, especially after the yeti had started their clandestine assault. And the strangeness of the natural sunlight, even if it was filtered by clouds, was liberating after being trapped for so long in the caves with only artificial lighting. Yet Herne could still sense uncertainty in the group, questions about whether they could succeed, whether the yeti could really be trusted, whether they had done the right thing leaving all the guards behind. Or maybe that last was only in his own mind; Herne suspected most of the others were perfectly happy with whatever comeuppance their torturers would receive.

It was still a challenging hike, though, even with the energy provided by the weeks of feasting they had enjoyed in the yeti's cave. They trudged along for hours on the side trail and then the road, pausing when anyone needed a rest but otherwise moving as quickly as they could. There would be time to enjoy the scenery on the way back, if they succeeded, and they didn't know when the engagement would begin. When they heard the first shot fired and saw an artillery shell take out a chunk of the rock face, forcing everyone to find cover, then they knew the time had come. Herne had never expected to take the Mavros guards by surprise—even with a night approach that would have been unlikely—but his plan didn't require that. He was just thankful that Aarn had been correct about the mine being defended by old-fashioned weaponry instead of silent, more accurate energy beams that would have been harder to avoid.

They regrouped around a corner, out of the line of fire.

"Okay, we've got the terrain advantage here," he said. Not only did it give them plenty of cover, but he could see the mine itself wasn't level enough for any helicopter pad, so he didn't have to worry about the soldiers there launching an air assault to defend themselves. Aarn had told him that, too, but he believed it now that he could see it for himself.

"They're sending out a scout vehicle," said Lei-Tan.

Herne nodded. "I see it. Let's go, no time to waste now."

Again, Aarn had been right, predicting that the Corsans would want a person involved rather than trusting a remote drone, which would have been difficult to maneuver through the mountain passes and easily evaded. Herne was prepared to shoot one of those down if needed, but skipping that step meant their operation would proceed faster, with less time for the city to be alerted and send support.

The roadblock was in place with a minute to spare before the vehicle arrived, one of the same trucks that had carried the prisoners to the mine so many months earlier, or at least the same model. The roadblock was simplistic: the yeti had placed a few small boulders in the middle of the road, not fully blocking it, but enough to force a vehicle to slow down, and Herne and Lei-Tan had run a rope across the way, anchored to the cliff on one side and held on a short pole on the other. The last part was to make it clear that this was not natural, so the scout would decide to stop and investigate rather than simply drive over or around the rocks.

And investigate they did, three soldiers stepping out of the truck, looking cautiously around. Herne wondered whether they were curious at all about what had happened to Herne and his comrades, or if they had simply assumed their vehicle had also fallen down the mountainside in the avalanche. If these particular soldiers hadn't been part of the convoy at the time, they might not even know there had been trucks that didn't make it. Regardless, they knew something was amiss here, and they were being careful, moving together, covering each other's blind spots. Herne also assumed there was at least one person still in the truck, providing additional protection.

Suddenly, a roar came from behind where Herne was hiding. It was a pathetic squeal of a roar, one that the soldiers would immediately know had come not from one of the monsters that they perhaps had heard tales of but from a boy teasing them. And just as Herne and Nika had anticipated, it made them relax their guard a little. At the same time, it drew their attention to where they had heard the cry from, and away from the other side of the truck, where three of the yeti followed the boy's instruction to sneak up on the guards and simultaneously slam them to the ground, immediately knocking them out.

Herne heard shots fired from inside the truck—only one shooter there, apparently—and he raised his own gun, leaned around his protective boulder, and fired through the windshield. The military-grade glass didn't crack immediately, not until the driver fired back at Herne, who ducked back into his hiding place. They exchanged a few more shots, Herne keeping the driver distracted until one of the yeti had reached the truck's door. Before the remaining soldier could turn to his side and re-aim, he was yanked out of the truck, his gun tossed aside and his body thrown over the cliff.

The first phase of the plan had been successful, but it was only the beginning. Herne had no doubt the contingent back at the mine had seen what was going on, possibly even watching a video feed directly from the truck. If not, they could all load in the truck, drive back to the mine, and pretend to be returning after successfully dealing with whatever troublemakers they had found in the pass. But he knew it wouldn't be so simple. In fact, they would be lucky if they didn't start to face heavy bombardment once the artillery at Mavros realized that their scouts were already dead.

"Okay, Lei-tan," he said. "Are you sure you want to do this?"

"Yes," she responded, her face betraying no sign of any internal struggle she might be facing. "My family is dead. My father-in-law took his own life for nothing; I'll make sure my death has a purpose."

Herne knew there was no time for a lengthy goodbye, though. Lei-tan got in the driver seat of the vehicle, yanked out the camera that she found on the dashboard, and smashed it to the ground, where a yeti crushed it under foot just to be certain. As soon as everyone else was hidden from view of the mine—making it easy for anyone at Mavros to assume they had all climbed in the truck—she sped off toward the mine, providing a desirable target for whoever was watching them. Meanwhile, Herne led the rest of them into the nearby cave entrance—not one that the yeti lived in, but one they had mapped out, which, if he and Nika had calculated everything correctly, would take them inside the boundary of the quarry zone, or at least to its edge.

Time was not on their side, though, and he didn't know how long Lei-tan would be able to distract the quarry guards. Not for the first time, he wondered if they could have just gone directly there, but the yeti didn't know of a way to connect their living quarters to this passage, and counting on getting there unseen, even at night, would have had its own risks.

So they ran, as fast as they could in the cave, relying on lanterns and headlamps for lighting since this tunnel lacked the electrical infrastructure of the one Herne and his group had been living in for the past months. They had the weapons that the yeti had stolen from the guards when they were first captured plus all they could find in the truck before Lei-tan drove it away. It was enough for nearly every human to be armed in some way, and most of the yeti were less interested in using firearms after the nearly disastrous first dinner; given their size and strength, Herne knew they wouldn't need them for the close-up fighting they would be doing. Most important, though, was the load of explosives they had brought from the stash the yeti kept on hand for whenever they needed to extend their caves.

The passage started to narrow, forcing them to slow down somewhat, but they kept up as much speed as they could while Herne tried to pay attention to the meanderings of the tunnel and how close they were to his target area. Skip the small opening to the left, follow a tight S curve right and then left. Was that the branch? No, the next one. Finally, there they were, just before the tunnel started dropping. If he was right, this hundred-meter section was directly under the command center for the mine, and close enough to the surface that he should be able to blast through. Nika helped direct the yeti as they set up their explosives along the ceiling, in what Herne hoped would be the optimum spot, and everyone retreated behind the curve.

"In three, two, one, blow!" he shouted, and one of the other men—Herne hadn't paid attention to exactly who took the controller—triggered the explosion, the stonefall temporarily deafening them while a cloud of dust nearly knocked them over, even at their distance. As the dust started to clear, they looked around the corner and could see light coming through where the roof had been; they had broken through!

Chapter 23

In Herne's fantasies, they had blown a hole right in the middle of an empty room in the center of the complex, with the fallen stone giving them a nice ramp to run up, get into position, and pick off the guards one by one as they came in to see what was happening. It was not going to be so easy in reality. In fact, the light was misleading, the dust scattering what were a few pencil-thin shafts of light to give the appearance of a full glowing opening. Still, they had blown through most of the rock, and once the dust had cleared, they could see the underside of the floor above them. And they could hear … nothing, maybe an occasional footstep, but not a mass gathering of armed soldiers. And certainly not echoes of the original explosion from grenades being thrown into the cave and quickly killing them all, as Herne had heard in his nightmares.

Nika, two of the yeti, and the smallest woman in the group —her name was Farrah, but Herne knew little else about her, like many others she had been reluctant to speak about her past—climbed atop the rock pile. When they felt certain they could hear nobody nearby, Farrah attempted to punch a small hole through the floor, using the butt end of her rifle and one of the larger chunks of rock that had fallen from the explosion.

There was enough of an air gap between the cave ceiling and the floor itself to have left a solid layer of concrete in their way in most spots, but she slowly chipped away at one of the thinner areas. Every bang made Herne wince, certain that they would be detected and their plot foiled. His only hope was that their noise would be masked by the other sounds of the mine, the pounding and crashing that he could faintly hear even down in the cave.

Finally, the floor yielded to Farrah's hammering. Seeing nothing, and hearing no reaction from above, she signaled Nika, who growled directions to the yeti. They quickly broke through a large enough area of the floor that Nika and Farrah could pull themselves up. Herne and the rest followed closely behind, lifted by the rest of the yeti rather than taking the time to scramble up the heap of fallen stones one by one.

In some ways it was better than Herne's fantasy: a narrow hallway about ten meters long with sharp corners at either end; they could hold the middle pretty easily as their opponents came around those corners. The major downside was the wall lined with windows, which looked out over the edge of the quarry. That meant the only soldiers looking their way would be on the far side of the mine, unlikely to notice anything going on inside until the shooting started and unable to do anything about it once it did, but it would give an opportunity for a broadside attack once their opponents realized that single file around the corners wasn't working well for them. As for the other wall, Herne had no idea what was on the other side of it. The interior of the building, for sure, but were there twenty soldiers in a briefing room there, armed and ready to start shooting through the wall? There was no way for him to know in advance, and Herne wasn't going to start shooting that way himself lest it be a boiler room or armory, or something else that could result in a massive explosion wiping out his entire group.

The last yeti was stomping up through the floor when two soldiers turned the corner and saw the intruders. The first was quickly dropped as at least three rifles were fired by Herne's companions. But the other guard managed to duck back without being hit, or at least not fatally, and, seconds later, an alarm sounded throughout the mine.

Herne's plan had only extended to getting into the mine area, knowing that the exact tactics to actually take control of it would have to be decided in the field, so now they were needing to go off book. After a quick consultation, they all agreed to split the group in two, half going to either end of the hallway. Farrah volunteered to lead the second half, and no one else objected, so Herne wished her luck and silently recited a Nupist thanksgiving prayer to Athena that someone else was willing to show some leadership.

They quickly moved into position; Jan faced behind at the back of Herne's squad in case there was a flanking move they needed to counter, and Aster took the same role in the other group. Just as they reached their respective ends, an artillery shell tore through the window, shattering it and then plowing through the wall into what turned out to be a restroom. It was immediately followed by two more, and Herne realized he had overestimated the importance of this building if they were willing to so thoroughly destroy it just to get at a small group of invaders. That meant he needed to get outside, fast, so he led his group around the corner, shooting down three more guards that were coming in, and reached the exit. He could only hope that Farrah's team had found their own path.

At the doorway, Herne could see that his calculations had been slightly off, and their cave had missed the main building. Instead, they had emerged in some kind of outbuilding, an oversized storage shed by the look of it, which explained why the soldiers had been willing to fire the artillery at it. The main command center was another fifty meters across an open dirt field that was by now covered by shooters in that building and others in vehicles parked around the field. A pair of soldiers tried to sneak towards the doorway carrying what looked like grenades, but someone behind Herne shot them before they could arm their weapons. It was a standoff, but it would remain so only until the artillery operatives managed to reposition their guns to safely aim at that end of the building without being afraid of hitting anything important. Or until someone called in air support from the city, which Herne knew couldn't be too far out.

It was one of the yeti that took action first, though, ripping the door off its hinges and using it as a shield while sliding along the wall toward one of the parked vehicles. Herne had the rest of his group focus their covering fire on the vehicles on the far side, to give the yeti as much of an opening as possible when he—or she, Herne still didn't know—needed to dart from the wall to the truck, holding the door straight in front but vulnerable from the side. The yeti's roar ripped across the field, drowning out the sound of gunshots; Herne couldn't tell whether it was a cry of pain from taking a bullet or a cry of victory, and he didn't dare to look until he heard two human screams following a second roar. When he finally did turn his head briefly, it was just in time to see one lifeless body thrown out of the cab of the truck and the yeti trying to squeeze into the driver's place.

Unfortunately, it was clear that the yeti had no idea how to operate the vehicle. Living in the caves hadn't given them much opportunity to learn human transportation technologies. It would have been comical, if Herne didn't feel like a dozen people's lives were depending on getting that truck across the field. He wished Nika was there, though the boy might have been too young to know how to drive anyway. One of the men with Herne—Bauman, a technician before he got swept up in a corrupt scheme and sentenced to the mines—started yelling directions to the yeti. It wasn't that complicated, if the yeti could only get it started, but between the noise on the battle-field and the yeti's limited understanding of human language, it didn't seem to be working. Finally, a second yeti picked him up and ran across the field, drawing fire from the Mavros guards. The yeti took a bullet, then another, and staggered bleeding until it was close enough to the truck to shove Bauman forward before it fell dead to the ground. The yeti in the truck moved over to let Bauman in, and he engaged the starter and quickly drove back to Herne's group.

There was no choice but to keep pressing the advantage, so once the truck was between them and any enemy snipers, Herne got everyone to jump in the back. He was counting on its armor to protect them as they drove across the field, just as it had kept Bauman and the yeti safe driving it over to them and prevented their bullets from hitting any of the soldiers in the other vehicles.

His thoughts about what they were going to do once they

got across were interrupted when he heard a cry from one of the men entering the truck behind him. Masud, slow in his old age, had been hit by a lucky shot—well, unlucky for him, Herne thought—that ricocheted off the wall as he was climbing into the back of the truck. It didn't look fatal, at least not immediately, but there was nothing Herne could do to help him.

"Don't worry, Masud. We'll win this battle fast and come back for you," he said as the man tried to crawl back through the open doorway to take cover in the building.

Herne strained to hear what the man mumbled back at him, knowing they might very well be his last words, even while he hoped that his own promise would prove true. He couldn't make them out, though, not with the overpowering noise of the alarm echoing throughout the entire site, blocking out everything but the sounds of gunfire and yeti roars. There was no chance to ask Masud to repeat himself; as soon as everyone was inside, the truck pulled away and headed straight for the main building.

"Shit!" someone cried inside the back of the truck. "Look over there!"

Herne, along with everyone else, turned and saw the huge tank that was coming onto the field from behind the building they had just left. Herne had never seen a model like this before, but then he had never really been involved in military operations, and city police forces on most planets had no need of such a weapon. He had seen pictures, in histories of old Earth, of similar vehicles, huge artillery mounted on treads that could traverse any terrain; he was sure the technology was more advanced here, but with Corsa's isolation, it might not have been that different. Regardless, it was a threat that he had no idea how to counter. Sure, their truck was armored enough to protect them against the rifles and handguns that were the most common weaponry here—intended for disciplining recalcitrant slaves, not defending the place against an invasion. But heavy weapons like the artillery that had blasted through the windows or the approaching tank would blow their vehicle up like a kid lighting a firework under a toy car. Not that there was anything they could do about it, though. They were driving as fast as they could move, and turning would expose their flank to the other guards.

The main tank gun boomed, echoing through the mountains, and Herne once more hoped that Castor had gotten away safely. But as he finished that thought, he realized that he shouldn't have had time to think it completely. He looked around and saw that one of the trucks that had housed some of the soldiers shooting at them was now a pile of molten metal and plastic, half-buried in a smoking crater. A second boom left the second truck in the same state. Then the top of the tank popped up, and a boyish head poked out, followed by an arm that gave a quick wave before ducking back into the protected tank body. Somehow Nika—and Farrah and the rest of the group, Herne supposed—must have taken control of the tank on the other side of the building they had emerged in.

A third blast from the tank ripped out the entrance to the command center just before Herne's truck reached it, the shock wave passing through and making it feel as if they were driving over a plowed field instead of smooth dirt. But the next person to emerge, from the side door rather than the now non-existent main entrance, had his arms raised and no visible weapon. Bauman stopped the truck in front of him, and Herne's crew jumped out, one of the yeti patting down the surrendering man and then throwing him in the back of the now empty truck.

"ERARU ERARU RECHUOUR!" the yeti roared, and that was enough to get three more soldiers to drop their weapons and walk out slowly, arms raised, following their comrade into the back of the truck. Herne led his group carefully into the building, wary of any remaining fighters that might be less willing to surrender peacefully. When he found the communications room—two comm officers immediately raising their hands and backing away from their terminals—he knew what he had to do.

Signaling to his group to continue taking control of the rest of the building, he went up to one of the comm terminals and tried to raise contact with Castor. There was no response at first, which he hoped was a good sign, that the *Umbriago* was far away, possibly out of range or simply far enough that he would need to be patient for a few minutes until the signal had enough time to travel there and back. He spent his time checking the net for any news about him or his ship. But there were no announcements of his imprisonment, no denouncements against Olympian infiltrators or declarations of war against any Olympian ships in the system. It was possible they were still waiting to see if Herne's lies about a fleet waiting just outside the system proved true, giving themselves an out to call Herne's incarceration a simple mistake rather than an aggressive act if they needed to. He was sure, though, that whatever their communication strategy had been so far, it would change once they got word of his actions here at the mine.

"Why am I not surprised you're alive," he heard a voice behind him. When he turned, he saw Gwen, handcuffed and being marched into the room at gunpoint by Aster.

"Sorry," said Aster, "she insisted on coming to see you, Tauno. Somehow she knew it was you leading the attack."

"Who else could it be?" Gwen continued. "No one else would be stupid enough to try it, or to think that taking over this facility here would actually be of any strategic value. Come on, now, take these cuffs off me. We're friends, right? Or do you have something else in mind for them?" She raised her eyebrows flirtatiously.

Herne shuddered. "I thought we were friends. You certainly didn't defend me when you had a chance, though."

"No, I certainly didn't. I could have, if you had told me who you were helping."

"Shouldn't we just kill her?" interjected Jan.

"No," said Aster and Herne simultaneously. Herne gave Aster a sideways glance and continued, "She'll be a good hostage here. Solomon wouldn't dare bomb us knowing she's here. That will give us time to get out. Just make sure you blow up the comm equipment once I get my message in, so she'll be stuck here for a long time."

Jan went over to help Aster chain Gwen to a pillar in the room, out of reach of anything that might be of any use to her. Finally, a response appeared on the terminal—not directly from Castor, but from the communications officer on the *Umbriago*.

"Herne! I'm glad you're alive," the response said. "Castor is no longer aboard the *Umbriago*. He transferred down to the planet. Here are the codes you can use to contact him."

Herne wondered what was going on—why would Castor transfer down rather than just leave? Was he somehow working with Rila, and if so, how did they get connected? But he noted the routing keys and sent a quick message saying he was alive and referencing the personal communicator that one of the comm officers was kind enough to allow Herne to take, after only a little threatening of his physical well-being. Then his attention went back to getting everyone clear of Mavros as quickly as possible.

He helped Jan and Aster chain up as many of the surrendered guards as they could, hoping that leaving them in the building would be enough to deter, or at least delay, an airstrike. He didn't have much faith that Oric and Solomon would care for those people's lives—even Gwen, despite her bravado, would be at risk—but every little thing that would shift the odds in their favor would be helpful. He left Jan to destroy the communication systems, and Nika and Farrah drove their tank to the work area itself, to let the overseers know who was in charge now. He didn't expect them to encounter much resistance; the fixed artillery there would still be at a disadvantage against the tank, and there was nothing left for the guards to win. Meanwhile, Herne went to help prepare all the trucks that hadn't been blown up. But first, he ran back into the doorway where Masud had hidden.

"Masud, are you there? We won!"

He heard no response, but he saw him, unconscious but still alive. Masud had managed to stop the worst of the bleeding himself, but there was still some blood seeping out onto the floor, and he was going to need serious medical attention soon if he was going to survive.

"I kept my promise, Masud. Stay with me," Herne said as he took a shirt from the first guard they had killed and used it as a bandage. He tried to lift him off the ground, but he was afraid he would end up making the man's injuries worse.

"Hey!" he shouted. "I could use some yeti help over here!"

Whether understanding Herne's request or out of curiosity, one of the yeti strode over and easily picked up Masud, carefully carrying him over to the back of one of the trucks, which was already filling up with freed slaves. Herne followed and helped load the trucks, sending them on the road as soon as they were full, as crowds came running from the mine, fleeing captivity while they had the chance. As soon as the tank returned, he laid out the next steps of the plan.

"Okay, Farrah, I'm heading back into the cave. Give me two minutes, then blow up the rest of the building where we came out, make sure nobody we missed tries to follow us."

"You don't want me to blow it up now?" she asked. "Get you in the last truck?"

"No, we need to check it out in case someone slipped in already," Herne answered. "I don't want them popping out and surprising us. We'll wait for you at the roadblock. You disabled all their artillery, right?"

"Sure did."

"Great. Anyone wants to come with me, you can, just be prepared to run fast. Otherwise, there are still a few trucks left."

With that, he hurried back to the tunnel entrance they had emerged from, trying to keep up with the yeti, who quickly passed him after Nika repeated the plan in their language. The walk back through the cave seemed much faster to Herne than

it had in the other direction, with a feeling of elation and victory replacing the anticipation and worry that had accompanied him that morning. It was still quiet, though; even if there
was less concern about being overheard and losing the opportunity for surprise, nobody wanted to talk about what they had
just been through. And there was always the worry that someone would be hiding, waiting to ambush them.

Chapter 24

Sybil had drifted off—she didn't know how long she had been asleep—when Pollux sounded an alarm to wake her.

"Sorry, I thought you would want to know right away," he said.

"Did the transfer succeed?" she asked as she cleared the salt from her eyes.

"Yes, but more than that. We have a message from Herne. He's alive!"

"What? Herne is alive?" Sybil shouted loudly enough that the neighbors would have heard, if the nearest neighbors weren't several light years away. "That's fantastic! Where is he? What is he doing?"

"I don't know yet," replied Pollux. "When Castor's transfer was complete, there was a message on the net encoded for him. He just confirmed with the ship that Herne had tried to contact him there first—too late for Castor to receive it, since his transfer was already in progress. But there's no current signal from him, and he didn't say exactly where he was."

"No signal? What does that mean?" she asked, bolting out of bed.

"Could be anything. Worst case, he's dead now, but that

would be a horrible coincidence if he was killed right after making contact. Maybe he lost his communicator, maybe he's underground. There is a report of some activity going on at one of the mines on the far side of the mountains from the city; it's a good bet Herne has something to do with that."

"Is he at risk there? What can we do to help?"

"Not much we can do if he's in a battle. We may be able to block a strike from the city, though. Weather's pretty bad, and as far as I can tell they don't have much of an air force anyway —no need for it, I presume. Some planetary defense missiles. You want to try to lock those out, just in case they aim them back down at him?"

"You don't need to ask me twice," said Sybil, excited that there was finally something for her to do. "Just set me up with a link to the Corsan net."

Sybil felt her pulse racing as she got her mind back into hacking mode. With more time, this would have been trivial for her, her array of social engineering tricks never growing old despite the centuries that had passed since she first trained herself to do this kind of work. But there was more urgency here than that would allow. If Castor knew something was going on at the mine, then the Corsan military leaders were bound to know at least as much about it as he did, and she had to block them before they decided to take action.

"You're on," said Pollux, having tied himself to her terminal input, with Castor passing through her messages onto whatever network he was connected to. Sybil tried not to think about exactly how this was working, the paradoxes it might induce, and what it meant to say that something had just happened at the mines when she was probably a hundred light years away. That was her eventual goal, of course, to under-stand the link, so she could take advantage of it, but for now, she needed to treat the whole scenario as just another job, prove that she could make use of the ems, and not get dis-tracted by the details.

She started out by probing the network around Castor, see-ing what he was connected to, finding any routing blocks or spies that might give her trouble. She thought the ninjas proba-bly had connections that would aid her here, but she didn't know where they would be able to, or choose to, instantiate Castor or how much access they would be willing to give him to their internal network.

"Yes!" she shouted to nobody in particular, forgetting that Pollux was listening to her every word, despite not being physi-cally present in the room with her. "He's inside!"

"I take it that's good?" Pollux asked.

"It helps, one less layer to worry about. He's got direct access to the agent I had them install earlier, when I edited the historical entries to foretell Herne's arrival. The military com-puters will have their own security, of course, but I've already bypassed the main government firewalls. Now I'll have no latency, so everything else will be much easier." Plus, she didn't say, it meant Castor—and thus herself—probably had full access to the ninja organization's network, giving her an oppor-tunity to understand more of its secrets. Those would certainly be of use to her wherever she ended up, independent of her ability to exploit this unique link in the future.

"That sounds dangerous for him," Pollux said.

"Hmm, it may be." She pondered the implications for a moment. "Probably no more so than a public network, though.

I'm sure they can shut those down at any time here, not like other, non-autocratic planets where that would be a lot harder. Quiet now, I need to focus."

She watched the traffic on the network, scanning for anything that looked like communications with a launch controller. The encryption schemes they were using were pathetic. Since whoever had received Castor hadn't put any restrictions on what she could run locally in the same computing fabric, she launched a serial quantum decryptor alongside Castor's emulation and was able to see everything plain as could be. If there was anything of value on this planet, she could steal it in no time. Then again, if there had been anything of value, she knew they wouldn't be spending all their effort on capturing human slaves; plus, they would have invested in more electronic protection. So it was lucky for her, or at least for Herne, that they didn't.

When the background port scan finished, she identified a handful of systems that looked like they may be what she was searching for. She hacked a login into the first two and learned nothing other than how bad their password protection was, but the third one was exactly what she was hoping to find. A few keystrokes, inserting a minor code modification, was all it would take. It wasn't that different than the fail-safe she had released into the Olympian system, after all, and this one only needed to affect a single central controller, rather than distributing itself to every ship connected on the network.

"There. Done." Sybil sat back, folded her arms, and let out a satisfied sigh. "All weapons launches should be locked out until they figure out what I changed. A few hours if they're smart, days or weeks if they're dumb. And given their isolation here, and their minimal experience with electronic hacking, I'd bet they're on the dumb side. Now what?"

"Now we wait and hope Herne gets back in contact. If he can rendezvous again with our other contacts, then we can figure out a way to get him back into the city, hopefully with more success this time."

Sybil didn't intend to just wait. She had more research to do. First, she needed to understand just what other government systems she could get control of: surveillance, doors, even sewer, anything that might be helpful for getting Herne back where he needed to be and making this mission a success. Beyond that, the commercial systems were of more interest to her. She hoped to find a way to adjust shipping manifests, identify valuable cargo—there had to be something other than slaves—and redirect it, either directly to her or to someone who would pay her well for receiving it. There was no guarantee that Castor and Pollux wouldn't notice, since anything she did would necessarily be linked through their own computing fabrics. Her simple safeguards would be enough to keep her side projects from being too obvious; she hoped that would suffice as long as she didn't give them reason to be suspicious. Luckily for her, Pollux was a trusting sort, the kind of em she had always easily manipulated. If she could pull off some kind of heist without them knowing while at the same time helping them with Herne—or helping them enough that they still trusted her—that would be the real success in her mind.

Chapter 25

They emerged at the cave exit without incident, most of the trucks already there and waiting, though not the tank yet. The trucks had been packed even tighter than they had been on the way out of the city; even with no guards taking up space, there had been many convoys to bring so many slaves to the mine and only this one to take them out. Nonetheless, the occupants all looked happier than Herne had seen on his ride out; they knew they were moving toward freedom rather than the opposite, and that made all the difference. Their faces changed, though, when they first saw him flanked by half a dozen giant furry creatures like they had never seen before. Many looked scared, but most seemed to take it in stride, just one more horrible thing that was no worse than what they had been subjected to in the labor camp, and a few even approached in curiosity.

Herne left it to others to do the introductions and explanations, though, as his new communicator signaled him the instant he was in the open air and had a clear signal.

"Where have you been?" came the voice in his ear.

"A long story, Castor," Herne sighed in reply. "Far too long to tell you now. Now we're in the mountains, though, and I'm afraid of an air attack. Do you think we can get safely back to the city?"

"I'm working on that. Missile launch codes have been scrambled. They'll figure out a way to do a manual override soon enough, but that might buy you a day. I can't stop planes or shuttles, but as long as the weather holds, you should be safe until you get to lower elevation."

Herne looked up at the clouds that still filled the sky, cutting off his view of some of the highest peaks, and hoped that Castor was right. He had never done much aeronautics—the cities on the planets he had lived on were always close enough to the space elevators or shuttle landing facilities that ground transportation was sufficient. If he had ever gone to Earth, that would have been different, and maybe some of the early colonies were already starting to spread out across their planets enough to require longer distance transit, more flexible than hyperloops. But Corsa was not one of those; while he had seen a few helicopters near the palace that would be useful to get over the mountains, they would probably not want to risk them in bad weather, and their orbital shuttles would be even less suited for military operations in this terrain.

"Okay. I'd like to hear how you scrambled the missiles, but that can wait, too, I guess. How about vehicle tracking systems? I told everyone to remove anything they could find, but all it takes is one to slip through and we're made."

"I don't know, but I'll try to get that blocked if it's not already."

"Are you with…," and here he lowered his voice to a whisper, though nobody was really paying attention to him, "Rila?"

"I haven't heard that name, but if I know who you're talking about, then yes, they secured my transfer down here before the *Umbriago* got too far away for ... well, that's another long story. Anyway, I'm safe here. What do you have in mind?"

Herne paused to think. "I haven't really thought that far. I've got ... not exactly an army now, but some people that have proven themselves brave and competent. And some ... other ... helpers. We'll need to meet up and coordinate, somewhere closer to the city, but still safe. Our mutual friend can contact me if she wants."

"I will pass on the message when she returns."

Herne then heard the tank approaching. "I need to go. Will talk to you soon."

"Be safe, Herne. And ... I'm glad you're alive."

"Me too, believe me," Herne laughed.

The tank arrived, and Farrah and Nika ran out.

"We found her," Farrah said, holding back tears.

"Found who?" asked Herne.

"Lei-tan. Her truck, or what was left of it, was halfway between here and Mavros. There wasn't enough of a body left to recognize."

"But we got the bastards!" added Nika. "Two trucks on their way back to the mine—they must have learned their lesson about only sending one."

"Yes," continued Farrah. "The artillery took her out, but they sent a group out to clean up any survivors. We ran into them not five minutes after we left, and now they have a few holes in them."

"Well, at least she died for a purpose. That was two trucks and a bunch of soldiers that we didn't have to fight at the mine. You never told me, though, how did you get the tank?"

"Oh, that was easy!" shouted Nika. "We ran once they shot out our window, and there it was, just parked outside the door! A couple soldiers were running for it—and I can see why they wouldn't want to be inside unless they needed to, man it was hot! But yeah, they were running, and they were going to beat us easy, but ORAREOR over there," and he pointed to one of the yeti, "he can move so incredibly fast! He got to the tank right when they did, smashed them against the side, and then Farrah and I ran over because there was no way he was going to fit in."

Herne certainly appreciated the boy's enthusiasm, but he had no idea how to tell ORAREOR or whatever his name was apart from any of the other yeti.

"You may want to keep a close eye on Aster," Farrah said in a lower voice, so no one else could overhear. "Maybe I'm paranoid, and I don't think Nika or anyone else noticed. She was guarding our back, after all. But before the race for the tank, I could swear she was trying to signal the soldiers. After we got the tank, of course, there was no further sign from her."

"Masud was worried there could be an infiltrator. You think it's her?" Herne asked, and he remembered her reluctance to kill Gwen and the oddity that she had brought her over to him in the first place.

"Like I said, maybe I'm paranoid. But I'll be watching her. You should, too."

The crowd was starting to grow restless, now that there was nobody left to wait for. There were well over three hundred people now, not quite the thousand they had thought possible, but many of them were in poor physical condition thanks to their forced labor. Herne estimated that only half of the people he had spent the night with in the Corsan prison cell were still alive, and that had only been a couple months earlier. The rest must have been from other convoys, either before or after his own. Taking them all back to the city would be like leading them into a slaughterhouse, but there was no way the yeti could care for them all, was there? Not for the first time—and he suspected not for the last—he wished he could communicate with the yeti himself, but instead he had to interrupt Nika, who was telling the tank story again to a dozen people that had come over his way.

"Hey, Nika. We need to talk to the yeti. How many people do you think they can house?"

"I'll find out," Nika replied, then he turned toward the group of yeti and yelled, "Hey ORAREOR! ORO ERARA RARA CHOERARAA!"

All Herne heard in response was a long growl, and he closed his eyes and shook his head at the idea that somehow Nika was extracting meaning from it.

"Either he's saying they can find space for most of them and feed them for ten days, or he's calling your mother a rotten turnip," Nika said. "Just kidding! It won't be comfortable, but given what they've all been through, it will still be a step up."

"Great, please thank them for me," Herne started to say, but he was interrupted by more roars coming from the yeti, which Nika needed to listen closely to.

"RAREOR," Nika replied. "They say their caves will probably be found now. Given what happened—and there's no way Solomon didn't hear about them from someone at the mine before we disabled their comms—he won't stop until they're wiped out, even if he has to completely level every single mountain in this range. So they are insisting they come with you to the city."

Even after the yeti had originally volunteered, Herne hadn't dared believe this was possible. "Tell them they are welcome! We can use all the help we can get."

"I already did."

Those who could walk marched the rest of the way to the main cave entrance, leaving more room for those who needed to stay in the trucks until they reached the side trail, too narrow for even the smallest vehicle. There, they camouflaged the trucks and the tank as much as possible, using rocks and the few dead branches they could find, hoping that it would be enough to conceal them from view through the clouds, even while knowing it would do no good at all from the ground. Herne realized that the yeti were right, there was no turning back for them now. With this many people knowing the location of their lair, the yeti's only choices were to kill them all or to join their fight and make a world that would hopefully be safe for human and yeti alike. He was glad they didn't choose the first option.

Herne helped as best he could, assisting one of the weaker miners into the cave, but the yeti took on most of the burden, their tremendous stride far outpacing any of the humans even while carrying two injured slaves on their shoulders. Herne remembered just how that speed felt when he was captured, though at the time it had quickly faded into a drugged fog. He hadn't even made it to the entrance when he heard a loud voice saying, "Welcome back, Herne!"

Aarn ran out ready to embrace him, then stopped and instead took the other shoulder of the man Herne was helping.

"A successful battle, I see?"

"Yes, a victory so far. But the war is far from over." Herne paused, then he felt he had to ask. "The other guards?"

"Taken care of. As promised."

"Dead?" Herne didn't want to leave any room for ambiguity. There were too many people who could be hurt now if any of the troublemakers remained. And if Aster was secretly one of those troublemakers, he would have to warn Aarn about her as well.

"Yes. Dead." Aarn didn't look too saddened by this, though Herne knew that they had been his coworkers and, possibly, at one time, his friends.

"There might be one more you need to keep an eye on," Herne continued. "I've heard rumors there might be an infiltrator."

"Yes," Aarn agreed, "there often is one, but I don't know if there was in our truck, and I wouldn't know who."

"We suspect Aster. Farrah and I both noticed some strange actions from her, though nothing obvious enough to call her out."

"I'll watch her carefully."

When they were all under cover, they made the arrangements. Nika seemed to get even more fluent as the planning went on, or perhaps the sounds he made were just blurring together more to Herne's ears. But he appreciated that the boy could still be so excited about his involvement in the preparations. They would all sleep here for one night—Herne would have to share his room now, of course—and those who weren't staying would leave in the morning, when Herne would finalize the meeting location. Over forty yeti would be joining, many more than had helped at the mine, and more than Herne even knew existed. He expected there would be about that many humans as well. Not much of an army, he thought, but with Rila and Castor, he hoped it would be enough.

* * *

"Okay, we're back in business," said Pollux later that day, far away from Corsa on the *Hispaniola*.

"He is still alive after all?" asked Sybil.

"Absolutely. I, or Castor, told him about your hacks of the launch system, leaving you out of it, of course."

"So he still doesn't know about me, then?"

"Correct, but that's going to have to change soon. It's time to get everyone together. We've set up a rendezvous between Herne and our local contact, Rila. He's going to need to know all our assets if we want him to contribute to planning our next steps."

Sybil didn't know how she felt about that. "How soon?"

"About twenty hours before they meet."

Well, she thought, it was going to happen. "Bring it on."

Chapter 26

The clouds had settled even lower by morning, with a mist filling the mountain passes. It was perfect, Herne thought, for sneaking back across the mountains without being seen from the skies. But it wouldn't stop a ground assault. A dozen tanks, and accompanying artillery, with his group trapped on a narrow mountain pass; it would be no contest. Still, Herne had two reasons for hope. First, whatever Castor had done to stop the missile launches might have messed with the rest of their military control systems. Second, perhaps the attack on Mavros would lead Solomon to think they were stronger than they really were, causing him to plan a defense around the city rather than an offensive move himself. Slim hopes, perhaps, but they were all he had.

"Are you sure we can trust these people?"

Herne had heard that question more than once, and by the time Nika asked him, he had an answer ready.

"Absolutely. As you know, my name isn't Tauno; it's Herne Sutherland." He watched for a flicker of recognition on his face, but as when he had confided in Lei-Tan, before sending her off to her death, there was none. "I'm not here as a trade representative. I came to find a way to undermine the pirate warlords here. It was a risky plan, I know, and by rights, I should have been blown out of the sky before I even touched ground on this planet. Somehow—someday I hope to learn exactly what they did—but I'm pretty sure the people we are about to meet were somehow involved in getting me as far as I did. Even though they launched the plot that got me caught, it wasn't their fault; sooner or later I would have done something like that on my own, and it might have gone worse. So yes, we can trust them."

Nika nodded. Herne knew it was a lot to ask. All these people who had been expecting to live in captivity until their last breath, now suddenly free. It was a reasonable instinct for them to want to scatter, to each find their own path. Even though the yeti had turned out to be helpful, that did little to raise anyone's confidence that the next group they relied on would be as trustworthy; if anything, it led the superstitious to feel that they had already used up their luck in that regard.

They loaded in the trucks and rushed down the mountainside as quickly as they could go, leaving the tank trailing behind them. There was no safety in numbers here; if they were attacked, they would be destroyed, so spreading out gave the best chance that at least somebody would make it through.

Herne was in the lead truck, and he followed the directions Castor had passed on to him, a series of landmarks that took him off the main road in the foothills and to an isolated patch of beach near the ocean, nearly surrounded by jagged cliffs that were perfect for snipers to keep an eye on any proceedings below. If he had been familiar with this planet's geography, he would have checked those out in advance, but he was certain that was the point; Rila knew the area, he did not, and she would make as much as she could of that advantage. He had followed her instructions to not share their destination with anyone else, thinking it was a rational precaution, especially if Aster was truly a mole, or if there was another one he wasn't aware of. If he had been willing to discuss it, perhaps one of the other locals might have actually been helpful, but that opportunity was gone now.

There was no one there to meet him when they reached the rendezvous point, so while the other trucks were starting to arrive, he contacted Castor.

"Hey, we're here," he said. "Where's my welcoming committee? Or are they going to bag us all and carry us into a dark room?"

"She is there," the em replied. "She needed to make sure you were not followed."

"And were we?" Herne asked. "I mean, I'd kind of like to know that myself, given that I'll be the first one blown to smithereens."

"It appears not. Once everyone is there, she will come out. Meanwhile, I suggest you stay down on the beach and not appear too interested in the rocky outcroppings looming over you."

"When did you get to be such a poet?" Herne asked, then he ended the communication, not wanting to hear an answer to his question, or to leave open a channel that might be used to track him or Castor any longer than necessary.

There was nothing to do but be patient until Farrah arrived with the tank, so he walked back and forth along the small stretch of sand, kicking the occasional rock into the surf. He had never been much of an ocean person, preferring the jungles and plains of Jurassia, or even the urban jungles of the various planets he had lived on before, to the endless openness of the sea. Even space travel didn't give him that same feeling. Sure, compared to a mere ocean, the openness of space was practically infinite, stretching without horizon, but he rarely had to look at it, and he was always confined within a ship, usually within a single room in that ship, and even that only for the rare times when he wasn't bound in a suspension chamber, completely oblivious to the vast infinities outside.

"Why are you off here by yourself?" It was Jan that finally approached him. "Come and sit with the rest of us."

Herne broke out of his own reverie. He saw a few others wandering on their own, and Nika was hanging out with the yeti, who looked completely out of place down here out of the mountains, their fur no longer needed for warmth or useful for camouflage in the snow. But most of the people had gathered on the beach by one of the trucks, chatting as if this were a mere picnic, despite the inappropriate weather for such an event. Herne could understand why they would be eager to get as much enjoyment out of this gift of time as they could, though; even a few days ago, none of them could have imagined being free like this, and they had no idea how short or long it might last.

"I would like that," Herne started. "Normally I would, anyway. I'm just nervous. I blew it last time with these guys. I don't want to get everyone else here killed, too."

"I get it. I'll leave you be. But don't carry it all on your shoulders. We all could have stayed in the mountains, you know. Or found our own way." Jan reached out as if to pat Herne on the shoulder, but instead, he simply turned and walked back to the group. Herne appreciated the effort, but it hadn't helped. Instead, it just made him more anxious for this to all be over, so that he could relax and go drink and laugh with people—these people, or people he hadn't rescued from a slaving mine, it didn't matter. He had never imagined that revenge would turn out to be so complicated.

Finally, Herne heard the rumble of the tank approaching. He half expected Rila to be following right behind, but he knew she would be smarter than that, not when the tank driver would be watching carefully, specifically making sure they weren't being followed. Instead, it was the yeti who noticed them first, after the tank had stopped and Farrah had joined the crowd on the beach. Their roars caused Herne to turn around just in time to see the last one emerge from a crevice in the cliff wall that didn't look like it could possibly there, let alone be wide enough for a person to pass through. Herne quickly ran to greet them, before any misunderstanding could take place.

"Herne Sutherland," one of the hooded figures said, and Herne strained to figure out which one was speaking. At least it sounded less threatening out here in the open, not echoing off the walls of a dark room. He looked back to see how many people might have heard, who didn't know his real name yet, but then he realized it didn't really matter now. No matter who they thought he was, given what he had done at Mavros, his fate would be instant death if he were caught.

"Yes. It's good to see you again," he replied, trying to address all of them at once.

"Quite an army you have now. We did not realize any yeti had survived."

That came as a bit of a surprise to Herne, that there was anything happening on this planet that Rila's organization didn't know about. But then, he knew they weren't omnipotent, or they wouldn't have needed his help, so he had no reason to assume they were omniscient.

"Well, they did. And they want to help," he added.

"Can you communicate with them?"

"Nika can." He gestured toward the boy, who was still sitting with the yeti but had stopped growling and was watching Herne's encounter intently.

"Good. They can't be stealthy in the city, I suppose, not like they can in their mountain home. But they will serve as a great distraction."

"It sounds like you have a plan then?"

"Yes, we do. We have a way to get you back in. And maybe a few of your most trusted associates here."

"While you stay hidden in the background, naturally." Herne grimaced. "In case we fail."

"Naturally," she replied. "But there is one more thing we can tell you now. You know that Castor is down on the planet now."

"Yes. He never explained why, though. I told him to get the hell out of here if anything happened to me."

"You know that he has a twin, as a result of the Eleusinian Totem."

"Yes, I was there when the cloning happened."

She lowered her voice, making sure that no one else on the beach could hear. "Do you know that they are quantum entangled? That they can think as one mind, no matter how distant?"

Herne's eyes grew wide. "No. What? He never told me that. But that means…." He paused to think through some of the implications. "Okay, I understand why he wouldn't tell me. If anyone found out and tried to take advantage of it. But you know about it…."

"Yes."

"And you're using that … how?"

"We needed someone to help with electronic infiltration. Someone with more experience than we could find here on Corsa, where, frankly, there is little motivation to learn those skills, no large payoffs possible from corporate espionage, only certain death if your first attempts are detected."

"And you found someone. But they needed to work remotely."

"There was no way they could get here in time. It is someone you know."

Herne racked his brain, but he couldn't think of anyone from his past that he had known to have exceptional hacking skills. "Who?"

"Sybil Vargas."

"Wait, Sybil?" Herne screamed after a moment of speechlessness. "That Sybil? The spy who helped Phoenix? She escaped?" Two of the yeti started to stand and come to his aid, but Herne quickly waved back at Nika that he was all right, and he got them to stop. "Why did it have to be her?" he asked, more calmly.

"We found her," she replied, unfazed by Herne's outburst. "She had arrived at a training center for our organization, not knowing what it was. I don't know the full story of how she got there. But Pollux was able to recruit her, and she has been helpful to your cause already, though you haven't known about it."

Herne thought about all the coincidences, everything that had gone his way to allow him to survive as long as he had on Corsa despite the slim alibi he had created for his arrival. Perhaps that had only worked because she had laid the groundwork for it, not because of his own skills at deception. But this wasn't the time or place to question his own competence; he could do that after they had won, accompanied by plenty of alcohol.

"Okay," he finally said. "I don't trust her, but I guess I trust you. Keep an eye on her, though. Now, what's the plan?"

Rila was silent, staring behind Herne. He looked over his shoulder and couldn't see anything unusual; all his people were gathered in the beach, with the yeti in their own group.

"Who is that?" Rila asked. Herne looked the other way and saw what she was looking at. Aster was off to the side, near the cliff, but not so close that she could be hearing their conversation. "She is one of them."

"Aster? One of who?" Given Farrah's earlier suspicions, Herne thought he knew the answer to this.

"One of Solomon's," Rila answered, matching Herne's expectation. Herne heard a whistle and sensed a quick movement from two of the people behind Rila, then he saw Aster fall to the ground. Herne rushed over to her, as did several others who had noticed what happened and were screaming as they ran. A pair of shuriken stars emerged from her throat, the artery severed and staining the sand red where she lay. On her wrist, a communicator—one she must have slipped from a guard at Mavros, the same way Herne had obtained his—was in an active session. Herne tried to take advantage of that, to learn who she was talking to.

"Is anyone there?" he yelled.

A tiny voice emerged from Aster's ear, but it was loud enough for him to recognize it. "Is that you, Tauno, my love?" Gwen. "Yes, I'm still here, chained up. I'm very disappointed with you, we could have had fun this way. I'll be seeing you soon, though."

Herne handed the device to one of the yeti, who smashed it between its hands. He wanted to take no risk that Gwen might overhear any of their plans. Farrah had come over at this point, looked at the body on the ground, and just nodded.

"You were right," Herne told her, though he could tell he didn't need to. To everyone else in the growing crowd, he added, "Aster here was the infiltrator. Jan had told me there might be one; Farrah suspected Aster, but we had no proof. My friends here recognized her, though, and took quick action. None of you have anything to fear, as long as you're not also working for Solomon. But we'll need to get moving quickly now," he said to Rila, "so tell us your plan."

Interlude

And the boy ran away from there as fast as he could, back to his parents' house, where he lived happily ever after." The child's mother tucked him in under the blanket and kissed his forehead. "Good night, Nika."

"Mom? Will the yeti really come take me away?"

"No, of course not. You're a good kid. Now go to sleep."

Nika paused to consider this. "But what if I'm bad some-time?"

"You're never that bad. Good night."

His mom walked out of the room, but his dad bent down and whispered, "Don't worry. The yeti aren't really monsters. They're friendly creatures, and maybe if you're lucky, you'll meet one someday."

"You really think so?"

"Anything's possible. Now go to sleep."

Nika did go to sleep, hoping to dream of a friendly yeti that would be by his side, teaching him to roar and play wild yeti games, defending him against bullies, and making sure he was never lonely.

* * *

"You're just a baby!"

"You still believe in the yeti!"

"Baby! Baby!"

The other boys had formed a circle around him, chanting while shoving him from one side to the other. At least they hadn't started punching him yet. They usually didn't, as long as he let them have their fun. He had made the mistake of telling his friend Mitja what his dad had said about the yeti being friendly and real, and one of the older kids had overheard him. Sometimes, if he got pushed in the right direction, he could see Mitja, cowering around the corner, watching, too small to come to his rescue but not willing to leave him to go get help— and Nika would never ask him why he didn't.

"You know what I'm going to do when I see a yeti?" one of the bullies started shouting in his face. "I'm going to shoot it! Shoot it right dead, and then shoot it again, blast it until all its guts are falling out everywhere, and then I'll cover you with yeti guts!"

"Yeti guts! Yeti guts!" the rest of the gang changed their chant.

"What do you think about that? You wanna be covered in yeti guts?"

Nika knew from past experience that silence wouldn't help him, so he eked out a quiet "No."

"Yeah, I didn't think so. So you better hope they're not real. All right guys, that's enough, let's go." With that, he gave Nika one last hard shove, and the other boys had backed off enough that he fell to the ground. "Bye, baby!" the bully called over his shoulder. "Remember: yeti guts!" Nika could hear their laughter echoing, and he couldn't see Mitja anywhere.

Chapter 27

A crowd had gathered, and it was growing larger by the minute. Children hid behind their parents in fear, or they tried to get a peek but were pushed behind because of their parents' fear. Whispers rippled through the growing assembly: "The yeti are back."

There were only three of them, not enough to be much of a threat as they walked slowly across the barren slopes toward the edge of town. From the time the first resident had seen them on the horizon and run back into the city to tell everyone he could, no more than an hour had passed. Unsurprisingly, there was a massive security presence—armed soldiers maintaining a perimeter, undercover agents on the ground among the crowd, snipers both visible and hidden up on the roofs and towers, all ready to shoot if needed. But the mob had grown too large too quickly for a quiet takedown; too many people were trying to rush out to greet the yeti, and the police were more focused on keeping them corralled than stopping the yeti from going further.

Then the news came: another small group of yeti was approaching the city, several kilometers further south. And soon there was a third cohort, each one drawing a similar crowd, and so many rumors that no one knew exactly how much to believe beyond what they could see for themselves. But one thing was clear: the city was shut down, not by decree or plan, but by reality. Too many customers had gone to see the yeti for the shops to remain open, and too many shop own-ers had done the same for anyone to be able to get their errands done. It was a holiday unlike any other.

As the yeti came closer and the crowds grew more forceful, Herne didn't know how long this detente would last, but he was certain that the tension would eventually break. One of the guards would shoot, and a yeti would be dead, followed quickly by the others in the group; they all knew that was the chance they were taking. Then chaos would ensue, or so he hoped, the crowd no longer restrained by fear, and everyone wanting to be the first to see up close, to say they were the one to touch the yeti. Either that, or the yeti would actually reach the crowds, and that would be even wilder. In either case, a convoy truck coming to keep control would be completely expected, and nobody would notice that they were coming from the wrong direction. Herne crouched in the foothills, out of sight of the city crowds and barely able to keep an eye on what was happening. Others had spread to watch each of the yeti groups, everyone keeping in constant contact with the other cells, so they would all be prepared when the status quo changed.

It was the second group where Herne's prediction finally came true. A young soldier standing on a sentry tower, arms shaking as these creatures he had heard of only in children's tales were walking toward him. Perhaps he saw a glint from the sun that looked like a weapon. Perhaps a particular childhood memory came back to him and caused his finger to squeeze the trigger slightly. But whatever the reason, the crack of the shot echoed off the mountains, only to be drowned out by the roar of the yeti that was hit and then more roars from its companions. Nika tried to translate, though Herne could scarcely believe there was anything there beyond simply cries of anguish that even he could understand.

"Let's go," said Herne as the roars were replaced by more gunfire until the yeti in that pod were silenced. He hoped that the other groups of yeti would stay safe, but they needed to hold their positions at least a bit longer, keeping the crowds engaged until reinforcements arrived. Farrah started up her truck as they rushed to the site, while other trucks, including the ones filled with armed yeti, headed to the two locations that hadn't yet had any shots fired.

With the yeti lying dead on the ground, the crowd had surged forward with such force that the police had no chance of holding it back. As Herne had expected, people had gathered around the corpses of the yeti, and more continued to stream in from the edge of the city. Soldiers were yelling, and occasionally shooting at the edge of the crowd, trying to get people to fall back as a pair of military trucks were making their way to the site. Or rather, three military trucks, including the one Farrah was driving, with Herne sitting next to her and Nika in the back with two others, Kami and Rowan. They slowly edged their way into the crowd, keeping their distance from the other trucks, hoping that nobody watching from outside would notice when they emerged from the vehicle without uniforms, and trusting that nobody in the crowd would care about them given the mythical creatures that lay before them.

They stopped not too close to the fallen yeti, where all eyes would be watching. Herne got a glance of them through the wall of gawkers, their red blood staining their white fur and the desert ground around them. He had seen them injured before, but even at Mavros, none had suffered anything serious, and he was glad he didn't need to go any closer.

Instead, the plan was to slowly make their way back to the city, surfing the waves of incoming bodies, expecting those bodies would pass by without noticing an occasional person moving in the opposite direction, maybe even being grateful that more space would be available for themselves. If Sybil had done her job, the surveillance systems would be offline, making it impossible for anyone inside the palace to be tracking them, or worse, recognize them. And the guards who were onsite were otherwise occupied with the general chaos of the crowd. Still, to be safe, they kept a good distance between each other, so they wouldn't stand out as a group.

Herne hadn't imagined it would be this bad, though, practically a riot. While it was true no one was paying attention to him, that was only because they were rushing past him so quickly he could barely keep his balance. Elbows and shoulders kept trying to push him back toward the yeti, and he struggled to keep any forward momentum as he weaved from side to side looking for open space to move. He passed more than one person lying prone on the ground, whether knocked over on purpose or by accident he didn't know; either way, the odds of them surviving without being trampled seemed low. They weren't Herne's concern, though; he needed to keep moving forward. He was so focused, he didn't realize that his group was one short until he heard the roars behind him.

"ARUARR!"

He didn't want to turn, but he felt compelled to anyway. He had moved far enough already that he could barely make out Nika's face, but he could see the tears glistening on his cheeks as he said goodbye to his friends. That probably would have been okay—any number of children in the crowd today would be sobbing at the death of these magnificent creatures, no matter how much their parents had played them up as monsters—but Herne knew the roaring was likely to cause a problem. If the soldiers thought it was simply an oddly loud wail, it might pass, but if they saw any hint of a connection between Nika and the yeti, it would not go well for him.

But there was nothing Herne could do, and he knew it. To go back to Nika now would only mean his own death and the failure of their mission—and hence the death of all the yeti. He turned away as Nika started up with his roaring again. Kami had nearly caught up to him; he could see Farrah ahead of him, also still moving, and he hoped Rowan was doing the same farther ahead and out of sight.

After a few minutes, he heard Nika's cries finally stop. He didn't dare look back to see if it had been voluntary or enforced, though. Nika didn't know many of the details of what Herne intended to do once he was back in the city, so Herne wasn't worried about him betraying them, but he still didn't want any harm to come to him. He hadn't heard any gunfire, at least, and there was no sound from the mob that might have been a reaction to new violence, so he remained hopeful that Nika might successfully escape and join them before too long. He tried to keep his thoughts away from what might have happened, though, and focused on what he needed to do, no matter how much he regretted allowing Nika to come on this most dangerous part of the plan rather than stay behind and support the yeti in one of the safer distractions.

When he was far enough into the city that the crowd thinned out, Herne could move more quickly. He felt like he had to, too, since any of the guards in the towers could still turn their head and easily see him now; if they recognized him, he would be dead before he realized he had been seen. But he made it into the maze of small streets that he had passed through on his first day out of the palace, astonished at how empty they were, and doing his best to avoid the gaze of the few people that looked out from their windows at the odd strangers moving away from the city edge rather than the direction that they had seen all their friends and neighbors running. This was not the way he had wanted to explore the town, and he swore to himself yet again that if he survived, he would come back and do it properly.

Before long, he found the building where Rila had first imprisoned him, squelched his instinct to look around and make sure no one was watching—a move that would have looked very suspicious if anyone had been—and went inside. He hesitated briefly as he crossed the threshold, expecting to be hooded or beaten or plunged into darkness, but it was nothing but an ordinary room, with Farrah and Rowan sitting on a bench waiting for him and Kami. There was no sign yet of Rila or her colleagues, but he knew they would be watching, waiting for everyone to arrive before they revealed themselves, and then the conversation he'd been dreading could begin.

Chapter 28

"That stupid kid!" Sybil shouted into the air. "Everything was going according to plan, and he had to go and make a scene!"

She was right; everything else had gone according to plan. She had followed up her shutdown of the missile targeting systems with a hack of the city-wide surveillance systems. She had left the palace grounds active—for now—to confuse anyone who was trying to track down the problem, but anything recording outside, including at the city perimeter, was swapped with a feed from some other camera and at a random delay. Somewhere, sometime, there would be a video display that would show Herne and his accomplices sneaking into the city, but nobody would see it today. And if someone fixed the system before it happened to appear—she gave them even odds of being able to do so—they might never see it at all. Even the hyperloop was unmonitored, although she knew there would still be guards onsite there.

But only four of the expected five made it to the meeting site, and Herne had reported that Nika had fallen behind, mourning for his precious yeti. That put everything else at risk. Sybil had wanted to leave the kid out of it, but Herne had insisted that he was the only one that could communicate with the beasts.

"I didn't pass that on," said Pollux. "I hope you didn't intend for me to." The linked ems had set up a voice channel for Sybil to participate in the strategy session with Herne and Rila, as the head of the ninja organization down on Corsa had introduced herself.

"Fuck if I care. If I don't want somebody to hear it, I won't say it out loud." Sybil paused as she had another thought. "Sometimes I wonder if I can even trust my own thoughts around here, though. Maybe you're quantum entangled with my brain, too."

"No, I'm not; we'd both know it if I was. And no offense, but I'm glad."

"Hey! Sybil!" Herne's voice came through, forwarded instantaneously across the light years. "Are you listening? How do we get in?"

"Asshole," Sybil said.

"Hey, I heard that!" said Herne.

Sybil would have glared at Pollux if there had been any physical location for her to glare at. She was stretched out on her bed, not even sitting at a terminal that would have given her a focal point for her anger. But then, she had just told him she didn't care if he forwarded everything she said, so she knew she had no right to be mad at him.

"I don't know why I'm helping you, given that you nearly killed me," she sneered.

"I don't know why I'm trusting you," Herne retorted in kind, "given that you would have happily shot me if you weren't so clumsy in zero gee."

Sybil wondered what everyone on Corsa thought about this. Her contacts must have known her history, after all—either from Esther or their own research—so they shouldn't have expected this introduction to go smoothly. But what about Herne's friends? This was all new to them, and they might be wondering what they had gotten themselves into. Not that she cared at all about them, but she didn't want to close off her opportunities for experimenting with the Castor/Pollux link by turning off her co-conspirators on the other end. She breathed deeply and prepared herself to play nice.

"Fine," she finally said. "You've got the map of the palace from before. Once you're close enough to the outer wall, I can track where you're going, and open doors as you need them. But keep in mind, they'll be able to track you, too. I don't have a way to do that independently of their surveillance system, and while I can try to obscure it locally, it won't take them long to work around that and capture the right feed."

"Okay," Herne replied, and here she imagined him looking around at Rila and her minions, hoping someone would give him a hint of what he was supposed to do. "Farrah and Rowan will form one party, go after Oric and any other lieutenants you can; Kami and I will go straight to Solomon, and then meet up after. And Nika, if he ever makes it here, can join us. Rila, you're sure none of your people will come along?"

"Absolutely not," came Rila's voice in reply. "Our organization must survive, no matter what. By the time you enter the palace, we won't even be in this building anymore."

"So in case we get captured, we're on our own. I get it." Sybil thought that Herne sounded remarkably calm about this, and she wondered whether Castor and Pollux might be processing the voices to mellow the emotional content, rather than just passing them through raw.

Just then, an alert came through on Sybil's side, one of the channels she had been monitoring in the background. Security forces were discussing a young boy that they were following through the city.

"Hey, just so you know," she interrupted, "it looks like Nika is being tracked."

"Is he headed here?" Rila and Herne asked at once.

"How the hell should I know? Is there anywhere else he would go?"

There was a moment of silence on the other end before Herne finally responded, "Probably not. His parents are gone, so he doesn't have a home he might go to."

"Is he smart enough to notice he's being followed?"

"He's smart, yes, but not experienced," said Herne. "He got rounded up for the mines, after all, within days of needing to survive on his own. Plus, he's not exactly in a great emotional state right now. I doubt he's paying close attention to anything."

"So we have to assume he will lead them here," said Rila. "We need to clear out."

"Will Castor be okay?" Sybil asked quickly. "You know I can't help you without him tapped in."

"He should be," Rila replied. "The computer grid is protected, and Nika doesn't know how to access it. Unless they decide to blow up the whole city block just because a boy went into an empty building, he'll be fine. But we need to make sure it's empty, so let's go."

"I've dropped the voice link," Pollux said directly to Sybil.

"Don't want to take the chance that they'll come in the building, hear us, and suspect something is going on."

"Of course."

"Do you really think they can take out enough of the leaders to matter?"

She thought about it for a second. "If they go quickly enough that people are still distracted by the yeti, they have a chance. Speaking of yeti, did you know about them?"

"My Castor side had come across some of the legends while researching on the Corsan network, but I don't think even Rila had any idea they were real, or still alive anyway, until they showed up at the meeting site."

"I'm glad we're headed toward a civilized planet. I'd hate to be down in that god-forsaken hellhole."

God-forsaken hellhole that was currently home to half of her secret treasure, she corrected herself silently, and she went through her plan in her own mind. She would help Herne and friends get through the palace, at least until they were deep inside and trapped. Once they were dead, Castor would beam back up to his ship, and she would gently encourage him to go somewhere he could be more useful to her. Then all the information she had gathered on Rila's gang would find its way to Solomon, and there would be fewer people around that knew what she had. Eliminating Esther—well, she was probably dead by now anyway, but her successors—would be trickier. She wasn't too worried that the secret would slip from them; if there was anything that organization was good at, it was keeping information to themselves. Most likely, Esther wouldn't have left any records, either, at least none that anyone coming after her would fully understand, but Sybil still wanted to avoid having anyone out there that might trace mysterious happenings back to her. If she was the only one that had a hint of how she was doing what she did, she would be much less likely to face more surprises like the men who had tracked her down in the Alaran space elevator. Meanwhile, she hadn't found a pirate ship to reroute or otherwise profit from, but there was no sign that Pollux had detected her work on that front.

"I know what you're doing," came an unfamiliar voice on the speakers in her room.

"What? Who are you?" Sybil looked around in confusion, though she knew it was one of the em crew and there would be nothing for her to see. "I thought Pollux had limited access to this room?"

"I'm the lead engineer, since Methuselah, er, Pollux took over as captain. You don't think I could find ways around his restrictions?" The voice paused, but Sybil didn't reply. "I know you're going to try to use their link for your own purposes."

"If you think so, why didn't you just kill me? You're Ani, right? The one that controlled my suspension pod? That would have been so easy for you to let that fail."

"I'm not a murderer, unlike you," Ani answered.

"That was self-defense!" Sybil interrupted. She assumed Ani was talking about the men who had captured her on Olympia, and then surprised her in a stairwell as she made her escape. Either that or her botched attempt to kill Herne, but it applied in either case.

"Plus, Pollux would have noticed, and he would not have approved," Ani continued. "But I'm watching you. And the comm ems know to block anything you try to send unless Pollux okays it."

Something had been bothering Sybil in the back of her mind throughout this conversation, and she finally realized what it was.

"Did you lead them to me on Alara?" she asked.

She waited for a response, but none came. That would have explained it, though. If Ani or some of the other crew didn't agree with Pollux on using her…. After her first visit to the *Hispaniola*, Ani could have easily sent a hint to someone on Alara that the notorious Sybil Vargas, most wanted hacker throughout the civilized galaxy, was there. She didn't know just how big a price there would still be on her head, but she assumed there would be some. She thought for a moment that she should tell Pollux about this betrayal by his crew, but she decided it wouldn't be worth it; it was far too likely that he would side with them and start to be suspicious about her motives as well, and she couldn't risk that. She would just have to be even more careful, and then figure out what to do about Ani after the Corsan job was done.

Chapter 29

Herne followed Rila's direction, running down the stairs into a cellar, then through a hidden door to a tunnel that appeared to split off into several adjoining basements but eventually led to a stairway that emerged into another vacant—or seemingly vacant—building. There was no time to waste; if the guards that Nika was unwittingly leading to Rila's organization's headquarters got curious, the underground maze might slow them down a little but not for long, especially if they brought enough people to fan out through all the branching passageways. Plus, he had no idea how secure this new site was, or if someone might stumble across them at any time and raise an alarm. So as soon as they were all out of the basement, they started leaving, Farrah and Rowan first, with Herne and Kami following three minutes later—just enough time, they hoped, to not draw attention to the fact that they were together, and to give the other pair a better chance if one was caught.

The streets were empty, though, as far as they could tell, and they saw no heads peeking out at them from behind curtains. Everyone in this area had gone to the edge of the city to see the yeti, and if the shooting had caused anyone to head home, they hadn't made it to this part of town yet. Even so,

Herne rushed to get to the palace walls, risking drawing attention to himself if someone was watching in order to get there
faster before reinforcements could arrive.

He didn't head for the main entrance—he knew that
would still be well guarded, no matter how many guards had
been diverted to watch the yeti and their attendant crowds—
but there was a service entrance through the outer wall on the
side near him that he hoped would be more accessible. Sure
enough, there were only two soldiers standing there, chatting
with each other, their guard relaxed in the face of a nearly
empty city. Kami, Herne had learned, had been an instigator,
trying to lead a revolution against the pirate warlords, but
unaware of Rila's organization. She had managed to acquire a
few guns and had trained herself to shoot before she was captured and sent to the mines, where she had been young enough
to stay in reasonable condition in the months she had been
there. Self-trained, then, but at least that was some kind of
training. From around the corner, she and Herne lined up their
shots and fired together, so as not to give either guard a warning. Two direct hits later, they ran to the door, to discover
whether Sybil would be doing her part and letting them in, or
if they would be stuck outside, waiting to be hunted down.

Kami tested it, and Herne was relieved to see that Sybil
had come through for them and the door was unlocked. They
carefully edged it open, wondering what would await them on
the other side, but there was nobody. Herne knew that
wouldn't last long—Sybil had told them that once they got
through the wall, they would be visible on the internal security
systems—but he hoped that with the minimal security at the
moment, reinforcements would have to come from the far side

of the palace, giving them time to move along if they were quick about it.

They darted across the courtyard, eyeing a loading dock on the side of the palace proper. The dock was closed, but that was good news as far as Herne was concerned, since it made it less likely there would be anyone there who might see them. They avoided the warehouse bay itself in favor of the side door that led to a hallway. He saw a light flip to green by the door just as they approached. It was either Sybil working her magic or someone on the inside coming out to attack them, but at this point, they had no choice but to continue, come what may. Herne flung the door open while Kami covered him, and he was relieved to find, once again, that their path inside was clear.

He ran into the maze, trying to remain grateful that there wouldn't be artillery blasting through the side of this hallway, like there had been at Mavros. The hard part, though, would be finding a safe path and avoiding being ambushed along the way. Luckily, he thought, he had help in that regard.

"Castor," he said into his communicator as he ran, "which stairwell should I head for?"

There was a bit of delay, and Herne cursed Sybil under his breath for insisting on having direct control of this part. If she had just given Rila, or better yet Castor, a direct feed into the security systems, he could have had a faster response. But she was the only one who could view it—because of some overly technical-sounding excuse that he didn't even try to follow because he didn't believe it was the real reason. Even worse, unlike earlier, when they were in Rila's building with Castor, the wireless communicator wouldn't allow a direct voice link, so all of his questions were relayed to her, and he had to wait for Castor to repeat her response.

"First left ahead, then just past a hall on your right is the door. Nobody in the stairwell now. Recommend you go up two floors—that floor is empty, too, at least in your area—and then check in."

He passed on the message to Kami, realizing it was probably worse for her, with him being one more link in the communication chain, but there was nothing he could do about that. When they reached the door to the stairwell, he stopped, opened the door slowly, and listened, in case the situation had changed or Sybil was misleading them. It was silent, so they leaped up the stairs as quickly as they could, and they had just about made it up two floors when they heard a door open and shouting above them. They ran out, knowing that they would have been heard but hoping that at least the floor they exited on wouldn't be obvious.

"Herne, Kami, we're in." Farrah's voice came across the communicator. Herne was pretty sure that was being routed through Castor as well—an unnecessary risk, it seemed to him, but Sybil had insisted that would be more reliable than using a direct wireless link inside the palace.

"Great," Herne replied. "Don't tell us where you are or where you're going, in case someone's listening. But how's it looking for you?"

"Looking clear so far."

"We've got company heading down to where we're at," Herne said as Kami silently pointed to an alcove across from the stairwell. He nodded—it was worth a shot, setting up an ambush if the soldiers they had heard entering the stairwell came out on this floor. The more security guards they took care of here, the fewer that could surround them later. "So we'll be out of comm for a bit. Good luck."

"Same to you," said Farrah.

Herne and Kami crouched into the alcove, waiting to see if the stairwell door would open. It seemed like it was taking forever, like maybe they had passed it by or gone out on a higher floor, but Herne knew he had to be patient, as it was just as likely they were taking their time to check every floor. Eventually, the door slowly opened, with nobody visible at first; they were professionals, not about to run blindly into a risky situation.

Two of the guards slowly crept out of the doorway, back to back, keeping as much of the hallway covered as they could. Herne expected them to step back into the stairwell once they saw the hall empty, but instead, the door closed behind them; they were leaving sentries on every floor, he realized. Kami signaled a countdown with her fingers, and the two of them each took a shot, direct to the guards' heads, felling them instantly. Not waiting to see if their opponents were actually dead, they sprang up and ran down the hall again, in case one of the guards had been able to issue a call for assistance before succumbing.

They managed to clear the area without incident, though, and Herne was about to contact Sybil for direction again, when he heard a booming voice over the intercom.

"Herne Sutherland!"

He froze, remembering yet again how Rila had captured him and repeated that name over and over. Then his eyes grew wide in terror as he realized that nobody here was supposed to know him by that name. Even Kami looked at him in confusion, not understanding why he was reacting in that way. Other than Rila and her crew, who had figured it out somehow, and Lei-Tan, who was dead, the only person he had told his true name was—

"Herne Sutherland! We have Nika Carmani in the basement security cell. You know the one. If you want to see him alive, you will surrender yourself there at once."

—Nika. They had captured him after all. He tried to think of a way to rescue the boy. He knew that simply going down to basement security—he assumed they meant the security room he had tried to infiltrate on his last day in the palace—and surrendering would be a trap. He would be killed immediately, and probably Nika would be right after; either that or he would be made to watch Nika die first and then be killed himself. Either way would be a disaster. Perhaps if Farrah and Rowan joined up with him and Kami, then they could overwhelm the guards, but there was no way they would have time to coordinate such an attack, and they would still find themselves cornered, likely to be crushed by reinforcements.

Kami was still watching him; she knew what it meant that Nika was captured, and she had probably figured out that Herne was his own true name, but she wasn't giving him any sign of what she thought they should do. Hoping he was making the right decision, he said, "We need to continue with our plan. There's no time for a new one, and our best chance to save Nika is to take out the leaders. They'll keep him alive as a hostage as long as they think there's hope to trap us, and if we succeed, we'll just have to hope that the foot soldiers aren't bloodthirsty enough to kill him out of spite."

Kami nodded silently—he couldn't tell whether she agreed with his reasoning or was simply willing to go along with him, but at least she wasn't arguing, which meant they could move fast.

"Castor, get me the next directions," he said into his communicator. "They've got Nika, so we've got to speed it up if we want a chance to save him."

Chapter 30

You're not going to like this," Castor said, "but you'll need to fight your way through to the next passage."

"I was afraid of that," said Herne.

"Keep moving; in about fifty meters, you'll turn a corner, then in another fifty or so, there will be a fire door. There's a squad of five coming from that way. If you can wait till they're through and get around them, Sybil can lock the door behind you."

Herne signaled to Kami and started running. He knew this section of the palace, a narrow passage that wrapped around the courtyard and connected the residential area to the offices. "Any chance we can tuck ourselves away in a room and let them pass by?"

"You can try it. They'll probably know you're there, though, and I can't tell if any of the rooms would give you more advantage than the hall. But don't be too slow; there's a larger group coming behind you, too."

"Of course there is," Herne huffed. "Don't worry, we're running."

Herne turned to Kami as they cleared the corner. "What do you think—fight 'em in the hall or ambush from a room?"

"These rooms," she answered, pointing just ahead and slowing down. "You take the left, I'll go right. We'll cover each other and hope at least one of us survives."

Herne could already see the squad coming around a corner ahead, so there wasn't time for discussion. "Sounds good," he said, and he pushed open the door to the left just as a bullet came whizzing down the hall.

The room Herne ran into turned out to be a storage closet. Its walls were lined with stacks of boxes—of what, he didn't waste time wondering. From the shots he heard across the hall, he gathered that Kami had not been so lucky in her choice of room. He didn't want to think about who might have been in there. Probably not pirates or soldiers, who would have been in the hall fighting already and wouldn't have let out such screams of surprise and fear. More likely bureaucrats, who wished they could have gone to see the yeti for themselves rather than being forced to stay at work, who might have been afraid something like this would happen when they heard the alarm. But he couldn't think about those people now; his priority was getting into a safe position before the security forces arrived. He also hoped that the larger group Castor had warned him about would be delayed by the dead bodies at the stairwell, and that the first squad wouldn't wait for those reinforcements to arrive, and that so many other things that were completely out of his control would go his way.

He quickly pulled two boxes away from the wall—whatever was in them, they weren't heavy, and that probably meant they would not be explosive, one more worry he had to push to the back of his mind—and set them up as a blind. Then he crouched behind them, giving himself a clear view of the doorway, and waited for it to open. He didn't have to wait long, and the soldier did a professional job of it, throwing the door open and jumping back to the side, out of the line of fire for someone standing in front of the doorway, but not for someone in Herne's position. He knew he couldn't wait; the boxes were such an obvious hiding place that the guard would be shooting holes in them within seconds. With his gun already pointed in the right direction, he hit the trigger, ready to take the man down. But the bullets were taken instead by a second man, who had run around from Herne's side of the door frame, trusting the first soldier to cover him.

This new man was further shredded as he fell by bullets from the man Herne had aimed at, who hadn't even waited to confirm that his partner was dead before shooting to protect his own life. Herne jumped out from behind his boxes, not trusting them to protect him once the falling body was out of the way. Sure enough, the boxes collapsed as they were riddled with holes, bits of foam and paper now covering the spot where he had crouched a moment before. With no more cover, his only move was to take the chance of crossing to the far side of the room, moving past the open doorway and hoping there wasn't a third guard covering his side of the hall. As he darted across, he got a glimpse of a guard lying still in the hallway and the final two standing with their backs to him. He tried to fire at one, but he didn't know if he had been on target before he lost sight, his back pressed tight against the open door.

He heard Kami let out a scream, and he seemed to hear one from the hallway, too; whether it was from his shot or one of hers, he didn't know, but he hoped that left only two guards in the hallway. Herne didn't hear the screams of the dying for long, though, as a louder sound came from outside the palace walls, carrying down the corridors and filling the space with one loud "NE'A ARARAUR!"

Herne knew what that sound meant—the yeti had made it through the hyperloop into the palace courtyard. That was the part of the plan that Herne had thought was least likely to succeed, not knowing whether there was any way to override the built-in security checks. And if he was actually starting to understand their language a little, they were looking specifically for Nika. For the remaining guards, though, it would be completely unexpected. This would be his best chance to escape from his closet, then, taking advantage of a moment of distraction on their part. It had come just in time, too, as he was starting to worry about how long it would take before the reinforcements arrived while he was still pinned down.

He slid along the door and rolled around the edge of the frame, firing his gun as he did so. He only needed a fraction of a second as the guard tried to understand the implications of the new sound, and he got it. He hit the crouched guard in the center of his forehead before the man could fire his own weapon at Herne, then he jumped into the center of the hallway in case the guard managed a stray shot as he died. There, a second person was lying dead now and the third was wounded, slow to turn around, giving Herne plenty of time to finish him off and be the sole survivor of this battle.

"Kami, are you alive?" he called. He couldn't tell for certain without going into the room where she lay, but she gave no response. All he heard was the whimpering of someone terrified and begging for their life, so he knew Kami hadn't actually killed the civilians, or at least not all of them. Behind him, he could already hear the footsteps of the group of soldiers coming fast, so he had no time to go check on her; alive or dead, Kami would need to be left behind.

"Castor, I'm clear," he said into his communicator as he fled the scene. "Get those doors closed as soon as I'm through."

"I'll get Sybil on it," came the response. Herne could only hope there wouldn't be too much delay, but he didn't need to worry. Even as he reached the doors, he saw the light on the control panel activate, and he was barely through when they slammed shut. Seconds later came the sounds of bullets hitting them; he didn't dare to look whether the heavy metal security doors were actually as bulletproof as he needed them to be. Instead, he kept running, even as the bullet sounds were replaced by human hands and what sounded like a makeshift battering ram hammering on the doors, plus a barrage of cursing and gunfire aimed at the control panel beside the door.

"Farrah, what's your status?"

"Can't talk now—in gunfight." Not Farrah, but Rowan had answered. He wondered whether Farrah was injured or dead, but he couldn't worry about that now. He had to get up this staircase to Solomon's level while he could.

"Castor, is the stairwell secure?"

"It should be," Castor replied.

"It better be," Herne mumbled as he went in and started racing up.

It was. Herne could hear more banging and shooting at the doors that he passed by on his way to Solomon's level, though. If Sybil ever lost control of the doors, there was no way he would be getting out alive.

"There's practically an army waiting for you on the sixth floor," said Castor. "We recommend you go up one higher. Then we can let them in and trap them all in the stairwell."

"And how do I get back down?"

"You're not going to like it."

"That bad?"

"Pretty bad." Castor paused. "You'll have to jump down."

"Jump? From where?" Herne ran past the sixth floor and could tell from the noise through the doors that he wouldn't be receiving a friendly greeting if he were to go out there. "Just tell me. I'm almost up there."

"The tank will blow a hole in the wall—"

"The tank is here? Awesome!"

"—and if we get it just right," Castor continued, "it should take out the floor between the levels. We'll have to time it carefully, so you're not so close to the explosion that the floor collapses underneath you, but you can jump down and get to Solomon before he evacuates."

"Sounds like the best plan ever," Herne said, knowing that Castor wouldn't be able to see his eyes rolling. "Wait, why don't you just blow him up with the tank? Save me all this work. Wouldn't that be easier?"

"We can't get it around to that side of the building. We could just start shooting left and right until we run out of ammo, try to bring the whole building down. But there are a lot of innocent people in there, and—"

"I know, I know," Herne interrupted. "You're right. And I'd rather not have to rebuild the whole palace when this is over; the new government, whatever it is, will need a building. So we go with your plan. But you're sure Solomon is still in his office now? I'd hate for this to just leave me trapped with nothing to show for it."

"Yes, he's still there, at least for the moment. And the seventh floor hallways are still clear; everyone has gone down to lower levels. Sybil should be opening all the stairwell doors now."

Just before Herne exited through his door, he could hear a mass of footsteps below, as troops rushed in from various levels. He wasn't so sure about the plan of trapping people in there. It sounded like there would be too many people to all be on the stairs, and someone would still be holding the door open; he didn't think Sybil could force the doors closed on them, only lock them if they were already closed. But that wasn't his problem. He just followed Castor's directions, waiting for the big kaboom coming from their tank, and listening to the sound of the yeti roars diminish, maybe because he was moving farther away from them or maybe because they had made it into the building themselves.

"Herne!" This time it was Farrah's voice that he heard, not Castor's. "Oric is dead!"

"What? Really? Are you sure?" Herne nearly missed one of the turns he was supposed to make, but he took a few quick steps back and corrected.

"Yes. And it wasn't us. It looks like your friends left a katana sticking out of his chest."

Herne was shocked. Rila's people had come after all? Of course that would be their style—to not tell him, so he couldn't betray them if caught, then take advantage of the distraction he was providing. Even Sybil hadn't noticed them, or hadn't told him about them if she had.

Farrah continued, "We have a bunch of guards here on the third floor that have surrendered. They seem to want to join us. Do you think we can trust them?"

"Why do you think you can?" Herne asked.

"They say they were just doing their job and are happy to switch to the winning side," Farrah replied. "At least some of them seem like they mean it. They're spreading the word through their secure channels that Oric is dead and that new commands are coming from us."

"Well, that would be a mess. How would we know who's on which side? Keep your eye on them; it could be a code message. But sure, use them as a vanguard and come up to the sixth floor; I'm sure I could use your help."

Herne waited a moment for a response but heard none.

"Farrah? Are you there?" He repeated a couple times, worried that the guards' surrender might have been a trap for them after all, but soon he couldn't hear anything other than the ringing in his ears, and he had a big view of the sky and the mountains through what used to be a wall in front of him. The tank had done its work.

"Castor? I'm going down," he said, but there was no response to that either, at least none that he could hear.

The tank had aimed high, it seemed, mostly hitting the floor he was on. So it was going to be less jumping, more squeezing himself through a gap that was barely big enough. He looked down once and quickly shut his eyes; he hadn't considered the obvious fact that he would be looking down to the ground outside the palace. He had seen the tank in that glimpse, though, and no pirate soldiers, so at least he was safe from there. But if anyone was left alive in the room below—or if anyone was to run in while he was dangling through the ceiling—he would be defenseless.

There was nothing to do but take the chance, though, so he slowly lowered himself down, maneuvering around wiring that he hoped wouldn't shock him and pipes that he hoped wouldn't scald him, until he had to let go and land on the floor. The room was unoccupied, as it had to have been for him to have made it this far.

"Castor?" he asked again, hoping to hear something now that his ears had stopped ringing, but still there was no answer.

He didn't need one, though. He recognized where he was from his earlier time in the palace, and he knew how to get to Solomon's office even without Ward as an escort. He carefully opened the door, but the hallway was empty, all the guards having gone toward the stairwells, whether or not they were actually trapped there. His legs were getting sore from all the running, but he kept it up until he got to Solomon's door, pushed it open and stepped aside as a bullet whizzed past where his head had been.

"It's you, Herne, isn't it? Or should I say Tauno? I knew you weren't what you seemed, and now I know that there is no Olympian fleet out there that I need to worry about."

"Have you heard? Oric is dead!" Herne taunted from around the corner. "You're next!"

He heard a deep laugh from inside the room. "Have *you* heard? Your little em—" Solomon spat, "is dead also. Now you're trapped here, and don't think those bear-men are going to be any help to you. There's a reason they were all killed or exiled; they're no good as soldiers. Surrender now, and I might let the Carmani boy live still."

Chapter 31

Wha happened?" Sybil cried after the long screech that had been reverberating throughout the ship finally halted. "I've lost my video feed. What's going on in the palace? Do we still have control of the door locks?"

She waited, listening, wondering whether the screech would resume. She knew it couldn't be anything good, but that left a wide range of scenarios, from merely bad to horrible. "Pollux? Tell me something! Please!"

She was just about to leave her room and try to get some of the other crew to at least tell her what was going on with their captain, when she finally heard a whispered response, barely audible in her ear: "I'm okay."

"You're okay, that's great," she said, trying unsuccessfully to keep the frustration out of her voice. "What about Herne? The palace? What's happening?"

"It's … I don't know." Pollux' voice was growing stronger but still sounded far from normal. "They got me."

"What do you mean, they got you?" Sybil was doing her best to keep herself under control, remembering her mantras from her time in the monastery, which all seemed so inadequate for the intensity that she was feeling now. Esther was right, she had missed this, the adrenaline rush, even when everything seemed to be going wrong. But that didn't mean she liked being so clueless about what was happening around her, or that she could stop herself from smashing something even though she knew that would do absolutely no good.

"There must have been a trace, back from the palace to Castor. Or maybe they just decided to take no chance after they had tracked Nika to the safe house, and they blew it all up after all." Sybil started to think—had she been so amateurish as to leave a link they could track? "But no," Pollux continued, "it wasn't instantaneous. They had him electronically isolated first, before they terminated anything running on the computing fabric."

"So, you mean Castor's gone?" She must have made some mistake, she thought. Maybe she should have let Herne and his allies have direct access to everything after all, rather than making Castor act as a proxy. She hadn't thought that would have made a difference as far as traceability, and she had just disabled their interface to Castor—without the em knowing, of course; she needed plausible deniability—so that Herne and his friends could be sacrificed, and she could get Castor to move to a more promising planet. But perhaps that had left some trace that she hadn't cleaned up, and that the Corsans had been able to follow. Just because their electronic security had been so laughably incompetent up to that point didn't mean they wouldn't ever manage to do something right, or at least get lucky.

Or possibly, she realized, she hadn't screwed up, but Ani had somehow sabotaged her sabotage; she couldn't imagine the em would have done that to her captain, but she didn't know what Ani was capable of, or whether she was competent enough to avoid a mistake like this.

"He's not on Corsa anymore," Pollux said. "I absorbed as much of him into myself as I could. But we're now just me. And just here."

Now Sybil understood the scream that Pollux had emitted. With the quantum entanglement, he would have felt every bit of Castor that was lost. And his attempt to expand himself with what was left of Castor—she didn't even know how that might be possible, but then, she didn't know how the Castor/Pollux link was really possible in the first place. But now that it was gone, she wanted to scream herself—all her schemes were impossible now, she would have been better off staying at the monastery, where at least she would have been safe from....

"I'm sorry for your loss," she said, "and I don't mean to be inconsiderate now, but what happens to me? You know there was someone hunting me just before we left Alara, right? Do you have any idea who that was?" She was tempted to mention Ani's involvement in that, but she decided it was still better to keep that to herself. "Are they going to be waiting for me at Sittian? Anything you can do about that?"

"I ... I don't know," Pollux replied tentatively. "I'm sure I can contact Esther, or reach the right contacts on Sittian myself. They'll know what you did for us. They can find a way to protect you, I hope." Sybil thought he didn't sound particularly optimistic about it, but given the circumstances, she didn't expect much. All she really needed was help to get off the ship and down to the planet safely. The days of keeping herself tucked away in a monastery, out of reach of any trouble, were long behind her now; it hadn't worked the first time, and she wasn't going to try it again. Instead, she could go into hiding on her own, fall back on the old habits that had served her well in the past, work her way back into the scene until her reputation was re-established. It wouldn't be the same as her grand plans to take advantage of the quantum-linked ems, but she would survive. And now, knowing such a link was possible, she would keep her ears to the ground for hints of another instance. Maybe, just maybe, she would have to plan her own heist on Eleusis—careful to avoid Phoenix's mistakes, of course —and see what other tricks the Totem might have up its sleeve.

"I hope so, too," was all she said to Pollux, though, and she started to head for her suspension pod. The pod that Ani would be configuring for her. She realized she would need a contingency plan if she was going to reach Sittian alive.

"Private conversation with Ani," she typed into the terminal after returning to her room. She didn't know whether Pollux would still be tapped into the audio feed, and she didn't want to take the chance of both of them being in the conversation.

"What?" came the response on the screen.

"I just want to let you know what I'm doing," Sybil typed. "There will be an encrypted message for Pollux, with a time-based key. I know what you did, and if something happens to me in the suspension pod, so will everyone else."

"Like I said before, killing isn't my style," Ani replied. "And now that you killed off Castor—"

"It wasn't my fault! You killed him!"

"I don't know what you're talking about. But now that you killed him off, the damage is already done. Still, if I decide I want revenge, there will be plenty of opportunity when we get to Sittian."

Sybil wished she had another choice than to entrust her life to this em, but even if there were enough provisions on board to last her to the end of her journey, and if she could manage to keep herself sane being trapped alone for so long, her body would be aged and likely dead by the time she arrived. So she had to take the chance and go into the suspension pod, where she could sleep until she reached Sittian, when the fun would begin again.

Chapter 32

Herne stood in shock for a moment, wondering whether Solomon was bluffing, or if he had really tracked down and killed Castor. It would explain why he had been suddenly cut off from communication, since even his link to Farrah and Rowan had been using Castor as a relay. On the other hand, there were plenty of other possible explanations for that, including Castor simply losing his network connection, not necessarily being terminated. But given how they felt about ems here, Herne knew there was no way they would let one live if they knew about it. And Solomon obviously knew about it.

There was one thing he could do to try and draw out the truth. He could still configure his stolen communicator for a direct link to his ship, rather than to Castor. "*Umbriago*, are you there? This is your captain, Herne." He realized that the ship was probably drifting further from the planet, so a reply might take some time. But he didn't want Solomon to know that, and he did want Solomon to hear what he was going to say next. "Castor is dead. Engage immediately with any Corsan vessels and destroy them. Then nuke the planet."

"You're not serious," Solomon scoffed from around the

corner. "Your ship would be destroyed before it could get in range anyway."

"Repeat, nuke the planet," Herne continued. "Don't worry about me, or anyone else still here. Nuke it, and get out of here."

"You're not really talking to your ship."

"I sent the message in the open. Check with your own comms people; they'll tell you whether it was really sent."

"Here, captain," came the reply from the *Umbriago* finally. "Message received. We will engage."

Herne hoped the threat would give him some sort of leverage: Solomon might not be completely confident in his fleet's ability to defeat a high-end warship. If there had been a human crew onboard, Solomon might have relied on his ability to persuade them away from such slaughter, but Herne was counting on the Corsan bigotry against ems making his threat seem more credible—even though Herne knew the ems would feel just as much guilt as any human about inflicting mass civilian casualties. Even so, Solomon was mostly correct; the odds of the *Umbriago* being able to pull off that kind of attack were not great. Any they sent now would be easily destroyed or redirected by planetary defense systems, so the ship would have to move a lot closer first, which would take days or weeks, depending on exactly where it was. That gave him plenty of time for him to call off the bombing if he was victorious, and plenty of time for Solomon's allies to destroy it if he wasn't.

But even if it only bought him a little time, that might be enough to make a difference. Herne knew Farrah and Rowan were on their way with a troop of guards that were, at least in theory, loyal to them now. Since Castor's demise would have taken away Sybil's control of the door locks, he assumed there would be a mass of guards coming from the stairwell soon, and there was no way to know their loyalty. Maybe Rila's people would be coming. Finally, somewhere out there were the yeti—close enough for him to hear their roars, maybe close enough and fast enough for them to join the fray. So even though there was no question Solomon had the better position at the moment, Herne knew he could probably wait out here until the inevitable battle royale. Still, he was hoping to be able to face Solomon alone first, and for that, he would have to come up with something that would change the scene.

"Look who's here," he heard from down the hall before he could think of anything. He quickly turned and fired, but there was no one visible, and the bullets simply buried themselves in the far wall. He had recognized the voice, however, even though he had only been in one conversation with it: it belonged to Arjis, the pirate captain who had been responsible for Phoenix's kidnapping in the first place, and the man who had foiled his original attempt to help Rila infiltrate the palace. He couldn't have been far from where Herne was standing outside of Solomon's office, but Herne couldn't tell exactly which room the voice was coming from, and he was afraid to think about how many others might be occupied.

"Don't worry about me, I'm unarmed," Arjis continued. "Just an old man biding my time here; I don't even care if you nuke the planet." He paused for a beat. "Yes, I heard that part, too."

He paused again, as if waiting for Herne to say something, but Herne wasn't going to let himself be distracted and let Solomon—or someone else unknown to him—come out and get the better of him. And he certainly wasn't going to take Arjis at his word that he was unarmed.

"So you're the great pirate hunter, huh?" Arjis went on. "The one that killed Phoenix? You should have said so before; I would have thanked you for taking out that bitch. Made a fool out of us by faking her death, she did, but you got her for real. You did, right? You're sure?"

Herne's face grew red, remembering how he had felt when Phoenix had died in his arms, but he still refused to give Arjis the satisfaction of a response.

"You know this floor is still sealed off, right?" Arjis continued. "Again, you were a great help, pulling them all into the stairwell. Then once we got control of the doors again, bang! No way were we going to trust them after Oric was killed. Solomon's got his own way out, though, don't you Sol, old buddy?"

That explained why Herne was still alone in the hall, he thought, rather than being overwhelmed by soldiers. He tried to figure out the dynamic here. He had assumed Arjis was on Solomon's side, but maybe he was just an old man, long retired from piracy and with no particular connection to Solomon, having received his commissions from earlier generations long since gone. But that left the question for Herne—who did he really want to seek his revenge on? The captain who had kidnapped Phoenix and set her on the path that led to her death by Herne's hands, or the leader of the system that enabled such kidnappings? Which would actually do the most to eliminate piracy in the galaxy, and which would make him personally feel better? And, of course, what did Arjis mean by Solomon's "way out"?

"Why don't you come out here where we can talk face to face, Arjis?" he asked, finally breaking his silence. "If you're really unarmed, I won't shoot you." He knew it was a risk. If Solomon and Arjis were coordinating, they might come out simultaneously, and he'd only be able to take down one. But they could do that at any time without his offering, so Herne figured the suggestion wouldn't really hurt him.

"Maybe I'll just do that."

Herne kept himself pressed as close to the wall as he could, eyes skipping back and forth frantically and listening for the sound of unwanted footsteps, until he finally saw Arjis step out from his room, hands up, and, to all appearances at least, unarmed as promised.

"You're not going to freak out if I put my hands down, are you?" Arjis asked.

Before he finished his question, Herne had already broken away from the wall and started running toward Arjis, accepting the risk that Solomon might come out and attack behind him. Not trusting Arjis's word, though, he quickly dropped into a roll. Sure enough, Arjis slid some sort of weapon out of his sleeve and fired right over Herne's head. Herne heard a grunt behind him and, as he rolled, saw a glimpse of a man falling— not Solomon, but he didn't have enough time to recognize the face as it turned away from him. Herne came out of his roll just in front of where Arjis was standing, threw his left arm in front of Arjis, pinning the weapon to his side, and rolled himself around to press his gun in the old pirate captain's back.

"No, your hands were better where they were," he said. "I only promised I wouldn't shoot you if you were unarmed." Arjis quickly dropped his weapon. Herne kicked it away and continued, "Sorry, that doesn't count. Still, I may need your help, so I'll keep you alive for now. Let's take a walk." He nudged Arjis along down the hallway, passing the dead body of what looked like Ward, who would have been Solomon's main lieutenant with Oric dead, but now had some kind of dart, presumably poison-tipped, sticking out of his neck. They stopped for a moment when he again reached the door to Solomon's office.

"Hey, Solomon," Herne said, "just to warn you, Arjis is coming in first. Whether you kill him or not is up to you."

With that, Herne turned the corner, keeping his head shielded behind the old pirate captain's. He could see Solomon's gun pointed straight at him, but he wasn't firing it, at least not yet, and that was all he could have hoped for.

"Your rule here is over, Solomon. Corsan piracy is over."

Solomon gave him a hearty laugh in reply. "No, no it's not. I'll shoot Arjis and you both—see, look at his face, not even shocked, he doesn't care. Your gang of wild apes will take over the palace today, but I'll signal the fleet to demolish the city if that's what it takes. Or just let your ship do the dirty work there, as you commanded. Either way, I'll find a pirate captain willing to convey me elsewhere, and we can re-establish ourselves on another planet. There will always be enough people who don't care for civilization, who prefer the frontier, and don't think all the pirates are really under my control, anyway. So even if you do kill me, it won't change anything. And now, goodbye."

Herne pushed Arjis forward just as Solomon fired his weapon. Arjis screamed briefly as a cascade of bullets ripped through him, but Herne managed to duck down in front of

Solomon's desk in time to not be hit himself. Whatever escape Solomon had planned, Herne was going to do what he could to block it, but first, he had to survive.

"Oh, well," said Solomon. "I guess I won't be able to kill you so easily. But still, goodbye."

Herne saw Solomon reach for something under his desk—he might have been activating an escape pod, a jetpack, or a shuttle attached to the window, Herne couldn't tell exactly. Then his attention was divided as he heard a crash from the hallway, followed by several loud, lasting roars. The yeti must have been strong enough to break through the doors to this floor, no matter how well Arjis had thought it was sealed. But if Solomon was really as close to escaping as he had implied, they wouldn't arrive in time to stop him. Even knowing that Solomon might have been right, that his own death or survival wouldn't make a difference in the long run, Herne wasn't going to let him go that easily.

He jumped over the desk as Solomon held up a small object that he had pulled out of his desk drawer, a controller of some sort. But Solomon turned his head to look down at the device in frustration while mashing harder on it with his thumb; Herne took advantage of the opportunity to knock it out of Solomon's hands and tackle him to the floor. He felt some kind of pack on Solomon's back as he had reached his arms around to grab him, and he hoped it wouldn't end up launching both of them out the window—more likely, he thought, it would be a parachute that would let him glide down into a remote-control shuttle—but whatever happened, he was going to hold on tight.

"I'm not even going to kill you," he said as he grabbed

Solomon's weapon out of his other hand and threw it to the same corner of the room where the control device had landed. "I killed Phoenix; I won't kill you. We'll put you up in a tribunal, have you answer for your piracy, your slaves, all your crimes. And then you'll be killed."

Solomon tried to push him away, twisting his body every way he could to loosen Herne's hold, but it didn't take long before the yeti came into the room.

"'ARRN! I mean, Herne!" said Nika. Herne wasn't surprised that the yeti had rescued the boy first before coming up to assist him. He was just glad to hear that Nika hadn't been killed down in the security cell.

"Careful," said Herne, "he's got some kind of escape plan. Through the window, I can only assume. The controller is in the corner behind me, but I don't know for sure what might already be activated."

Nika went over to the window and looked. "I don't see anything out there." Then he picked up the controller. "And I can't tell what this does. Are you sure he wasn't bluffing?"

Herne stared into Solomon's face for any kind of sign, but all he saw was a face staring blankly back up at him, betraying nothing. "Who knows. Can you send a couple yeti over here to give me a hand, though?"

Nika roared and signaled to two of the yeti, who came over and pinned Solomon to the ground, giving Herne a chance to stand up. He backed away, not wanting to be too near as they grabbed the pirate warlord, each holding one arm, and lifted him up completely, feet dangling in the air. In the last moment before Solomon's feet left the ground, though, he quickly shifted his weight just enough to be able to reach into a pocket with one hand; he pulled out a slender knife and thrust his arm back, jabbing the blade into the belly of one of the yeti holding him. Without hesitation, but with a roar unlike any Herne had heard from the yeti before, the beast ripped Solomon's arm away from his body, knife still in hand, as Herne could only watch in horror. Solomon screamed in agony and blood spurted from the wound, and Herne quickly grabbed Nika and ran out of the room, not wanting to be a witness to what he knew would be coming. He was slightly disappointed that his plans for a tribunal had been foiled, but he felt no real sadness at the fate Solomon would meet.

Chapter 33

A ren't you going to the parade?" Nika asked.

Herne sat in his old quarters in the palace. It was little changed in the months that he had been gone—no one had even bothered to remove his personal belongings—though he felt like it had been a lifetime since he had last been there.

"No," he answered. "I'm happy here. Let the Corsans celebrate."

"You could be a Corsan, you know," said Aarn, who was sitting in the corner opposite Herne.

"I know. And you could be in the parade. After all, you promised you'd come to the victory party."

"And I came, didn't I? But no, the parade isn't the place for me."

"Are you afraid of retaliation?" asked Nika. "There hasn't been anything like that against any of the guards that came over to our side at the end. And you were there even earlier."

Aarn didn't answer. Herne thought he understood the complicated emotions his friend was feeling—ones that would make it difficult for him to celebrate a victory over what had until recently been his life's work—and he knew that Aarn wouldn't want to try to explain them to a boy like Nika.

"Have you agreed to police the city during the transition?" Herne asked, trying to change the subject.

"Yes, that Rila can be … persuasive," Aarn answered. "Until there is a new government established, I said I would lead the police force, as small of one as we can get away with. But once there's someone else who can take over, I'm retiring. So, like I said," Aarn added, moving his right hand in a circle, beckoning Herne to follow his logic, "you could be a Corsan."

Herne laughed. "No, thank you. The last thing I want is to be responsible for Gwen's trial."

"What happened between the two of you, anyway?"

"It's … complicated." He glanced at Nika. "And that's all I'll say about that. At least we learned how Solomon was planning to escape, though."

"Yeah, it's lucky Mavros is that far out, or maybe unlucky that Aster had managed to alert a rescue truck for her. But if she had arrived just a little earlier, Solomon could have done his parachute evacuation before you even got to him. I would have liked to be there when she was trying to negotiate her way past the yeti though."

"That would have been interesting, I'm sure, but I'm glad I missed it. Anyway," Herne continued, "I've already got the *Umbriago* coming back into orbit—they know about Castor, which was a big loss, but the rest of the em crew is ready to go. As soon as my shuttle is back in working order, or I find another one that is recovered from whatever Sybil did to ground them, I'm heading back on board and then back to Jurassia."

"Dinosaurs!" Nika interjected. "That's so cool!"

"Yes. Yes, it is. And it's about time I get back there. I'm

sure it will be completely different from when I left. But I've had enough of this Pirate Hunting business. Someone else can take over that title from me, and they can get the ship to go with it. You go enjoy the parade, though, Nika."

After Nika said his goodbyes and ran off, Aarn continued the more serious discussion. "You really don't think there will be problems from Corsan ships returning? It could be a hundred years from now, they could have a load of captured slaves already, and they won't be happy if we tell them there's nothing for them here."

"Oh, I'm sure there will be problems. You'll need to get the word out as soon as possible that slave ships are no longer welcome here. Any that come, their passengers will automatically be granted Corsan citizenship when they disembark—or offered passage back to wherever they were heading before they were kidnapped. You'll have to use your judgment on the ship captains and crew, whether they can be trusted to switch to a more civilized career or need to be imprisoned. And some, I'm sure, like Solomon said, they'll find some other planet out there. Until the whole galaxy is populated, there will always be some frontier they can use. But there's nothing you can do about that." He stopped and grinned. "Well, other than hiring a Pirate Hunter, I guess."

"And if they decide to 'nuke the planet'? This one, I mean."

Herne laughed again, then held his sides against the pain that hadn't yet faded. "Yeah, you'll need some defense against that, though there already are some ground defense systems in place. Solomon was right that I was bluffing there. Well, mostly bluffing. But Olympia or any other planet would be happy to sell you upgrades. Add a couple ships to patrol the system and shoo away any troublemakers, and you're set."

"And an experienced Pirate Hunter to lead those ships?" Aarn asked hopefully.

"You said a hundred years. It could be much more, but even at a hundred, it's not going to be me the whole time—unless you keep me in suspension, with a sign to open only in case of pirate emergency. And there's no way I'm agreeing to that, so you might as well put someone else up there from the beginning. Hell, get a yeti to do it."

Now it was Aarn's turn to laugh. "You know, not a single one wanted to stay here in the city. Nika said they were all happy in their caves and just wanted to live in peace on their own."

"I can't say I blame them. But I'm sure Nika will keep visiting them. Maybe you'll make him an official ambassador or something. And other kids—or people much better at languages than I am—will follow him. And who knows, maybe some yeti kid sometime will get an idea to explore the rest of their world, or even beyond."

"Yeah," Aarn replied, "it will be the kids. Always the kids."

"Yes, it always is," said a female voice. Aarn and Herne both looked up to see who had slipped into the room without them noticing. Herne was not surprised at all to see Rila's face, still partially hidden by her hooded cloak, despite no need that he could see for her to go incognito. "And that's why we do this, too. For them. So they can grow up in a better world."

"And so they never have to see their parents kidnapped and dragged off into slavery," added Herne. "But now, you've finally achieved your organization's goal—after how many years? Do you think you can really make a smooth transition here?"

"Yes, of course. We have a long history of ... shall we say, running things."

Herne grimaced. "You do know that controlling things behind the scenes is not the same as setting up an open government, right?"

"We're not stupid, you know. But you're sure you don't want to stay and help? There's a long tradition of war heroes leading democratic transitions, you know—George Washington, Charles de Gaulle, Ming Xiaowen ... Herne Sutherland?"

"War hero? Me?" Herne scoffed. "No way. This was hardly a war, and I was never a hero. And even if Aarn twisted my arm and made me stay, I wouldn't know the first thing about governing."

"You can always read Plato," Aarn said with a laugh.

"Anyway," Rila continued, "I just wanted a moment to thank you, Herne, for helping us. And Aarn, when you're ready, you know where to find me." With that, she turned and left the men alone in the room.

"What do you think, Aarn? Odds on whether this turns into a disaster?"

"I'll do what I can until the day I die," he answered. "After that, I'm gone, you're gone, and all bets are off."

Acknowledgments

Thanks to everyone who read *Methuselah* and told me it wasn't horrible. Particular thanks to Allison for her ongoing encouragement, her suggestion that the book include yeti, and introducing me to Gwen, plus all her other help in making this book better.

David Peterson's *The Art of Language Invention* inspired me to try to work out a realistic yeti language, even if no human will ever be able to speak it. The language itself is all my own, though, for better or for worse.

About the Author

Ron Stieger lives in Seattle with his wife and two sons. A hardware engineer by day, he is a graduate of Caltech and has designed satellite systems and coffee makers, and lots of things in between. He is the author of *Methuselah* and several short stories. He definitely thinks pirates would win if the ninjas didn't have the yeti on their side.